The Diary

The old man stared into my face with his filmy blue eye.

"You look a lot like the girl who used to live here," he said. "The one who's dead."

The word *dead* sounded like a rusty door hinge.

"I've never been here before," I said, becoming more afraid.

"I think you have," the old man said.

As I backed away, he continued to follow me, step by step.

"Don't you want to know how she died?" The man smiled … an eerie smile.

I took a deep breath. "What happened?"

"She was murdered … by one of her friends."

Look out for:

THE *Point Horror*
DIARY

Sinclair Smith

■SCHOLASTIC

Thanks to hairstylists
Michelle Ramin and Sandy Calemine for technical advice

Scholastic Children's Books,
Scholastic Publications Ltd,
7-9 Pratt Street, London NW1 0AE, UK

Scholastic Inc.,
555 Broadway, New York, NY 10012-3999, USA

Scholastic Canada Ltd,
123 Newkirk Road, Richmond Hill,
Ontario, Canada L4C 3G5

Ashton Scholastic Pty Ltd,
PO Box 579, Gosford, New South Wales,
Australia

Ashton Scholastic Ltd,
Private Bag 92801, Penrose, Auckland,
New Zealand

First published in the US by Scholastic Inc., 1994
First published in the UK by Scholastic Publications Ltd, 1995

Copyright © Dona Smith, 1994

ISBN 0 590 55926 5

Printed by Cox and Wyman Ltd, Reading, Berks

10 9 8 7 6 5 4

THE
DIARY

Point Horror

Chapter 1

Let me tell you how I died. I remember seeing blood before my eyes. At first I thought I was floating in blood, but then I understood that I was lying in water, and the blood was swirling in the water around me. I knew that it was my own blood, but strangely enough, that didn't bother me. I felt quite calm and peaceful.

That's when I realized that I wasn't breathing anymore.

"Wake up!"

"Delia . . . please wake up now. . . ."

Voices ripped through the thick fuzzy blanket of sleep that I'd drawn over my head. I pulled it tighter around myself. Inside its warmth was safety; I could sleep on, and still hide from my nightmare.

It was awful. In the nightmare I had been

reading about someone's death in a diary. *And the handwriting was my own.*

After I had read the words, I had slammed the diary shut, and not been able to move. I thought I was dead.

I would never forget the way the diary looked. It was red, with a design swirled on the cover. *Like blood swirling through water.*

I tried to curl tighter into sleep.

"Delia!"

I felt myself starting to awaken. I resisted.

"DELIA, YOU'RE SCARING US! PLEASEPLEASEPLEASEWAKEUP!"

I heard the edge of fear in my friends' voices, and allowed myself to rise from sleep.

As I started to awaken I remembered that this was my eighteenth birthday. My best friend had thrown a surprise party for me at her house, and afterwards a bunch of girlfriends and I had stayed to sleep over. We had all been talking about the party, our boyfriends, etc. I must have dozed off.

I opened my eyes, expecting to see my friends' smiling faces.

But instead, everybody looked so scared — with drawn, tight expressions.

Apparently they were worried because it had taken so long to wake me up. And I'd been talking in my sleep. I told them that I'd just had a bad dream, and I'd tell them all about it later. Right now, I wanted to write it down.

I grabbed a pen and pulled out my diary.

There was a chorus of booing, and teasing comments.

"Come on, let's leave her alone."

"Do you believe she brought that thing to a party?"

Someone threw a pillow at me.

Although the dream still scared me, I couldn't help giggling. My friends always teased me about writing in my diary so much. But I knew the teasing was good-natured.

I'd been keeping diaries since I was a kid. I happened to mention it to my English teacher, Mr. Parrish, and he suggested that I try to write the diary the way I would a novel. He said it would be good practice if I wanted to be a writer one day.

I didn't know if I wanted to be a writer or not. In fact, I really didn't know what I wanted to be. But I followed Mr. Parrish's suggestion anyway, and wrote my diary as if I were writing a novel. A true novel about my life.

Right before I put the pen on the page, a thought occurred to me.

"Hey, you guys . . . when I was talking in my sleep, what did I say?"

"I don't know what you said exactly," one of my friends called out, "but your voice sounded like it was coming from the other side of the grave."

Chapter 2

"Papaya Passion, or Tangerine Tease?"

A strange voice seemed to come out of nowhere, filtering into my mind which was tangled in the web of last night's nightmare. It was the same nightmare I'd had on my birthday sleepover two days ago. I'd had it three nights in a row, now.

"Papaya Passion, or Tangerine Tease?" said the strange voice again.

"Hey, Delia, what's with you? What kind of drink do you want?"

I recognized this second voice as belonging to my best friend, Judy Diamond. The sight of the rows of bangle bracelets on her wrists and rings on her fingers reminded me that her nickname, "Jewel," was perfect for more than one reason.

I pulled myself back to reality. Now I understood that the question about Papaya Passion and Tangerine Tease was coming from the little speaker in the happy clown head at Bonzo's Drive-in Restaurant. I stretched across Jewel, reached through the car window, pressed the button on the clown's tie, and said, "Papaya Passion."

Bonzo's was getting an early start on summer with their "Tropical Festival." Every week they featured two of their "exotic" juices. Bringing a little flavor of the islands to the perfect little town of Pleasantville, U.S.A., I thought ruefully, gazing out the car window at the mini-mall where Bonzo's was located.

I could see that the trees planted in little patches on the mall sidewalk were waving slightly in the faint breeze. The warm spring air smelled clean.

"You're getting the Papaya Passion? I think Tangerine Tease is much better," Jewel said, tossing her black hair over her shoulder with a flip of her bangled wrist.

Just then an obviously disgruntled employee in a Bonzo's costume trundled out with our drinks and a huge fruit salad. Eyeing the getup the Bonzo's staff was forced to wear, I couldn't blame him for looking unhappy. Besides a clown costume, everyone at Bonzo's also had to wear the symbols of the theme of the week. Wearing two brightly colored flower leis, this poor guy looked like a sad-faced clown caught at a Hawaiian luau.

"Where did *that* come from?" I asked, pointing to the salad that I recognized as a Bonzo's Tropic Volcano for Two. *It's erupting with fruit,* the menu said.

"I ordered it for us, remember?" Jewel maneuvered the tray holding a hollowed-out watermelon half filled with fruit onto the seat in between the two of us. "I asked you about it and you said, 'fine.' Anyway, it's my treat."

Jewel's bracelets glinted in the sun as she paid for lunch. "Dig in! We've got twenty minutes before we have to be back at school — and I think this fruit salad might be a little . . . excessive."

Jewel took a long sip of her drink through a bright orange straw. "Ummmm . . . you can almost taste the tropics!"

"You sound just like a TV ad," I told her, laughing. For a moment, laughter had chased away my somber mood — but only for a moment.

Jewel nudged me lightly. "Hey . . . tell me what's bothering you. You look like somebody died."

Somebody did. Me. I frowned at the grim joke as I watched Jewel pick the slices of lime off the fruit salad. She hated limes.

"Jewel, remember the sleepover on my birthday — when I dozed off and you woke me up?"

Jewel nodded. "You were talking in your sleep . . . in that voice." Jewel laughed nervously. "It was so weird . . . but then you told us about the dream you had. You were just talking that way because you were having a dream."

Jewel laughed again. It didn't sound any more convincing the second time.

"It wasn't just a dream — it was a *nightmare*. And last night, I had it *again*. It was *exactly the same one*."

"You're reading the diary of someone who is dead . . . and the handwriting is your own, right? You said the diary had a red cover."

"Right."

I turned to look at Jewel and I saw my reflection in each of her eyes. Like two shiny pictures of myself, I thought. Jewel was waiting for me to continue. I took a deep breath.

"You know why that nightmare is so frightening? Because it didn't feel like any nightmare I ever had. It felt like it *really happened*." I spread both hands out, palms up, and shrugged. "And you know what else? Ever since I had the dream the first time, the strangest things have been happening. Uh . . . what is it when something happens and you feel like it's already happened to you before, and now it's happening all over again?"

Jewel looked puzzled for a moment. "Wait a minute . . . oh, yeah. Déjà vu." She shrugged.

"Right. I get feelings like that. I feel like I remember things that I know never happened to me."

Jewel poked the fruit salad with her spoon, shoving pieces of fruit around. "Like . . . what kind of memories?"

"Well . . . I was standing in front of Morton's Shoe Store the other day, and I remembered buying some red shoes for the prom . . . just as clear as day. But Brock and I just went to the prom, and I know very well I wore a cream-colored dress with shoes to match . . ." I let my voice trail off.

At the time the memory felt so *threatening*. But I realized that saying I had thought about shoes didn't *sound* scary.

Even before Jewel started to speak, I could tell from her expression that she didn't think so, either. "That's not so terrifying. And there are plenty of explanations. Maybe you just wanted red shoes. Or maybe you wished you wore *red* to the prom. I get the feeling you think it all means something, but I'm not sure what you think it is."

I felt a swell of frustration. But how could I expect Jewel to understand . . . when I didn't understand myself?

"Well — I'm really not sure *what* to think of all this. Maybe thinking about buying a pair of shoes doesn't sound scary. But having memories that aren't my own makes me feel afraid. So does dreaming that I wrote about my death in my diary . . . after I died. . . ."

I stopped talking and leaned forward, putting my elbows on the dashboard. Jewel was looking thoughtful, as if she was considering what I said carefully.

"That stuff sounds like something straight out of a horror movie, all right," she said finally, and glanced at me out of the corner of an eye. "I think it's interesting that you dreamed you read something in a diary. But of course, it makes sense, because you've always kept a diary. Even when you were a kid, right?"

Jewel knew that was true, and she didn't wait for me to answer before she continued. "Are you sure that college isn't what you're worried about — and that's what's making you feel scared, and giving you nightmares? It's senior year and you still haven't decided where you're going."

"I'm not afraid of going to college," I snapped.

"Okay," Jewel said quickly.

I leaned back into the seat and crossed my arms. Jewel backed her red Jeep out of the parking lot, swiveled it around, and eased out onto Lakeview Pike. We started back toward school, cruising along past the medical center, the Keenway's Cut Rite Shoe Store, and the Saucy Pig Barbecue. Except for the Saucy Pig, these few buildings had all sprung up within the past five years. Sparsely dotting Lakeview Pike, they represented the modern section of Pleasantville. A meager effort at that.

I gazed out the window, lost in my own thoughts. Though I didn't want to admit it, I knew that what Jewel said made sense — certainly it made more sense than thinking you were getting some kind of message through your dreams. And it was true that I hadn't been able to decide on a college yet . . . but lately something had changed.

Now I not only couldn't plan for college, I couldn't imagine anything taking place in my life any farther in the future than this summer.

Every time I tried, I got scared. Really scared. And it was like my mind ran up against a brick wall and just . . . stopped.

I knew I couldn't explain it to Jewel . . . it was something I didn't understand myself. But lately I was beginning to think that I couldn't plan for the future . . . because I wasn't supposed to have one.

Chapter 3

For a while, Jewel and I drove in silence.

"I'm glad I'm going to be going to college, and getting out of Pleasantville," Jewel said finally. "I mean — and don't get me wrong — I've been happy growing up here in Small Town, U.S.A. — but how many places are like this picture-perfect little town? It's like — it's like being in a straightjacket."

"A picture-perfect straightjacket," I echoed. "That's an interesting comparison, but I suppose it fits Pleasantville, all right."

I knew exactly what Jewel meant. I'd lived in Pleasantville all my life, too — well, almost all of it. Both of my parents were killed in a car accident when I was very young. They died instantly, or so I was told. And then I'd come here to live with Aunt Gracie, my mother's sister.

I tried hard to understand my aunt, and not

to dislike her. But it wasn't easy. Aunt Gracie certainly didn't live up to her name, for there was nothing *grace*ful about her. No, thoughts of Aunt Gracie brought to mind stiff, starchy fabric, and harsh soap. The stuff of minding your manners and being quiet and serious, prim and proper.

Aunt Gracie never went out without wearing her short white gloves. She always wore a dress, never slacks . . . and in the hottest weather she wore stockings. Not pantyhose . . . *stockings*. Aunt Gracie's biggest — in fact her *only* — frivolity was her hair. She had it dyed in the blue rinse even old ladies seldom wore anymore.

Aunt Gracie didn't nag me about going to college — in fact, she went to the other extreme. She thought that I should get a job here in Pleasantville and spend the rest of my time taking care of her. As far as she was concerned, college was a luxury that I could find a way to pay for myself. I didn't know how I could do that.

I liked it here in Pleasantville. It was comfortable and safe, unlike the wide world out there, where I had no idea what to expect. But staying here meant being around Aunt Gracie. So in the end I was always afraid to leave Pleasantville, and afraid to stay, too.

Even though I was in a car, I couldn't help glancing around, as if Aunt Gracie would somehow be there watching me. Just the thought of Aunt Gracie made me feel like a guilty child.

"You know — Pleasantville is so small-town perfect it's *unreal*. You never read about places like it in magazines. *It's eerie*. There are all these social issues — and nothing's going on in Pleasantville." Jewel shook her head. "You know — it's like a show I saw on TV once. A man is about to crack under the pressure of his job, and one night when he comes home on the train he passes through an old-fashioned town like Pleasantville. He decides to get off and stay there. Except the train doesn't pass through any such town . . . only in his mind." Jewel glanced over at me. "Are you listening, Delia?"

"Yeah, Jewel. I'm listening," I said absently.

I didn't exactly agree with Jewel. We passed a billboard on the roadside. On it was a picture of a man in some kind of uniform. The caption said, *I'm always here to help,* but someone had written in another caption of their own in black spray paint. It said, *I'M A REAL SICK-O.* Right beside the billboard was a HOP 'N STOP convenience store, spanking clean, except for graffiti on one wall that said *YOU'RE ALL KILLED DEAD.*

Well, I thought, open your eyes, and there's plenty of evidence that there's something brewing beneath the surface of pleasant little Pleasantville.

Jewel turned onto Chesterfield Road. Harding High was located at the end of it. Chesterfield Road was more of a long dirt path than a road, though. As I shielded my eyes from the glare of the sun I could see us approaching the dull brown one-story structure of the high school.

Harding High had been built shortly after World War II, and was clearly showing signs of age. Outside it was made of dark-brown-colored bricks. If I had to describe the architectural style, I suppose I would have had to say, "none." Inside, however, was another story. That, I would have called "early dungeon."

We pulled into the parking lot with time to spare, and joined the others who were trying to find spaces in the undersized lot.

"Change your life by taking advantage of the golden opportunities in the travel industry. Train at home!" an advertisement blared from a car radio.

Now, there's an option, I thought as I hopped out of the car and slammed the door. "You have to phone us! We can't phone you!"

the announcer said with excitement that seemed to border on hysteria.

Jewel and I hurried toward the building as hordes of other students poured in. We were all in the same boat, I thought. It was a strange time of year — a limbo between Senior Prom and graduation. Everyone was just drifting — spending time with friends they'd be leaving in the fall, thinking about their new lives ahead. And I was more in limbo than most of them. I sighed with resignation as I pushed my way in.

Students rushed along in the dim cavernous hallway that served as a perfect echo chamber for the laughing, noisy crowd. Sounds of shouts, whispers, and guffaws bounced off the walls, ceiling, and metal lockers. I made a quick stop at a drinking fountain, and then hurried to class.

The day sped by. In spare moments, I silently tried talking myself out of my fears. I told myself that I was only a victim of my own wild imagination. By the time I stopped by my locker before my last class, I had almost convinced myself.

I dialed my locker combination, spun the lock, and swung the door open. I was rummaging around for the book I needed, when something on the top shelf caught my eye.

A card.

I opened it.

In bold, sharp, handwriting that cut into the paper — more like a slash than a scrawl — was written, *MAYBE THIS WILL HELP YOU REMEMBER*.

I turned the card over. There was no signature.

What on earth did it mean?

And then I saw it. Sitting on the top shelf of my locker, tied with a red ribbon, was a book.

I reached up and took it off the shelf.

As I held it, time whirled to a stop for me, and in the noisy hallway the sounds in my ears were silenced.

The unreal had become real.

This wasn't an ordinary book — it was a *diary*.

With a red cover.

I'd seen the same diary before.

In my nightmare.

Chapter 4

My eyes locked in a tug-of-war with my powers of reason.

It was *impossible* that this was the diary I had seen in my dream.

But I couldn't deny that I held it in my hand.

The very sight of it hypnotized me.

As I held the diary I felt a *presence* — of something.

Or someone?

Alive.

Or dead?

The *thing*, or whatever it was, touched me. I felt the touch through the diary — on my hand, and right through to my mind and down into my soul.

So this is what the *kiss of death* is like, I thought.

I dropped the diary as if it had scorched my fingers.

I felt sick to my stomach.

Students milled about in the crowded hallway, oblivious to the fact that among them was someone electrified with fear. Shock wave after shock wave flashed through me like lightning.

I couldn't move — and I couldn't pick up the diary. I just stood there in the crowded hallway, trying to keep hold of my sanity.

A scream was forming deep inside my chest, already forcing its way out. But just as I was about to scream . . . the cry froze in my throat.

Suddenly, I felt very foolish.

Of course.

It must be a present from my boyfriend, Brock. It was our six-month anniversary. And I had been so preoccupied that I had completely forgotten.

I bent down and picked up the diary, embarrassed at the way I'd dropped it on the floor. *Kiss of death,* indeed. *Have you lost your mind?* I scolded myself.

Poor Brock! He'd dropped hints like crazy for a while. No wonder he had then started acting so moody. A sigh escaped my lips.

"Hey, Delia! See you in class!" a voice called out to me. I turned to see a petite blonde in a cheerleading outfit. It was Brenda Ann

Bandy. Brenda Ann never seemed to have a worried day in her life.

"Yeah, Brenda," I said, and smiled as she walked by. Jewel and Brenda were both pretty and popular, and had carried on a friendly rivalry for years. Still, I wondered for the umpteenth time if Jewel and Brenda were really just kidding around when they made those sarcastic remarks to each other. It wasn't the kind of humor I liked.

I started to put the diary on my locker shelf, but the cover was so unusual I took a moment to examine it. It's really *maroon,* I said to myself. Not the same color as the one in the dream at all. The design on the front looked like it had been hand tooled, and the cover was soft.

An antique? Well — maybe not that old. But not new. It was the sort of thing you'd find in a curio shop that held a jumble of secondhand books and pieces of mismatched china, and maybe a really beautiful carved music box and a lamp that once belonged to somebody's grandmother. It was the kind of shop I loved to haunt.

I'm a lucky girl, I said to myself, thinking how thoughtful Brock had been to pick out such an unusual and special gift.

As I examined the design on the cover more

closely, I realized that a monogram was cleverly worked into it. Unless you looked closely, you wouldn't even notice it. The letters curled and circled around each other in a way that could have been simply a decorative design.

How clever! And *I* had spotted it.

I strained to make out the initials in the monogram. It looked like LL — or was it LR? No, not LR — it was definitely LL, I decided.

I tried to imagine what sort of person LL was. Surely it was someone who was serious about a diary, to have one as beautiful as this! I didn't think I'd ever seen one so beautiful. Perhaps LL had been as devoted to keeping a diary as I was.

How strange to know you shared an interest with someone you'd never met, I thought. I wondered if LL and I had anything else in common. I looked down at the diary, and felt a twinge of fear I couldn't explain.

Chapter 5

I looked up and saw Brock and his friend Timmy Sweeny strolling down the hall toward me. Timmy was laughing aloud, and gesturing with both hands. He was like an overgrown kid, and always seemed on the verge of running into something or knocking it over, and yet he never did, except when he played football. There it was an asset.

Brock's lean, muscular body moved along smoothly, with just a trace of an arrogant swagger in his walk. In worn jeans and a faded T-shirt that clung to the curve of his shoulders, it was easy to see why girls found him attractive. His brooding, dark eyes gave him a romantic, mysterious quality, but they often twinkled with mischief. At first glance of the duo, though, no one would guess that Brock was the one who was the famous school prankster.

Brock was full of contradictions. That only made him more interesting to girls, it seemed.

As the duo came to a stop in front of me, Timmy cuffed Brock lightly on the arm. "I'll figure out a way to get back at you one of these days, Davidson." Then he turned to me. "You'll never guess what your bonehead boyfriend pulled after gym class."

Brock put on a face of mock innocence and shrugged his shoulders. I looked at Timmy's grinning face. "No, I can't guess."

Guys got a kick out of Brock's pranks. As far as I was concerned, sometimes they were funny and sometimes childish and annoying.

"What I can't believe is that you figured out my gym locker combination," Timmy said, shaking his head. They both laughed. For a moment, they reminded me of two rowdy six-year-olds.

"Magic hands," Brock said, giving me an obvious leer which I pretended to ignore. I shook my head. Sometimes what guys got a kick out of amazed me.

"I know you're both dying to tell me what happened, so go ahead."

"Davidson somehow snuck a kitten into my gym locker. So, after gym, I dial the combination and unlock the locker . . . but I don't open it. Then I take my clothes off so I can take a shower."

I was wishing Timmy would finish the story, but he was obviously enjoying himself. From his expression I could tell he thought he was being quite entertaining.

"Anyway, I'm standing there buck naked, and I pull the door open to throw my clothes inside . . . and the kitten leaps out. Wo! Was I surprised. In fact it scared the — well, it scared me a lot. Scratched me up a little, too."

Brock was grinning even wider now, and Timmy started laughing again. He stopped when I didn't join him, and the grin slowly vanished from Brock's face.

"What did you do with the kitten then?" I asked Brock.

"I put it back outside." He shrugged. "Well, don't look at me that way, Delia. There's a cat out back of the guys' locker room that had some kittens. I put it outside *gently*. It's not like I threw the thing out the window. Its mother was out there."

Timmy, sensing something was wrong, said a hasty " 'Bye!" and was gone.

"That kitten must have been scared to death inside that locker! What were you thinking of?"

Brock stared at the floor. He looked like a guilty child.

"Well, it was only in there for a minute. I did it right before class ended and everybody came back to the locker room."

Brock looked up at me, and strands of dark brown hair fell over his forehead. "But you're right. It was really stupid and . . . thoughtless. I was just doing anything for a laugh." He smiled at me, showing a single dimple in the left corner of his cheek. "Come on, don't be mad at me." He kept smiling as he stared into my eyes.

He was deliberately turning on the charm, I knew. And we both knew it was going to work. As often happened, Brock could change from a bratty little boy into a romantic character in less than an instant.

Brock crossed his arms and leaned against the locker beside mine. His expression was serious, but his eyes sparkled gleefully. He continued to look at me, as if inviting me to share in a private joke.

We stood there for a moment, and then Brock leaned toward me, put both arms around my waist, and pulled me close.

He felt warm, and I could feel his heart beating inside his chest. I reached up to touch his hair where it curled a little at the base of his neck. I knew he was going to kiss me . . .

"Ahem! Good afternoon, Delia. Brock. It's getting to be time for class."

"Oh! Thanks, Principal Tucker." I jumped away from Brock.

"Thanks, Principal Tucker," echoed Brock with obvious insolence. As soon as the principal passed, he pulled me close again. I could smell the soap from the shower he'd just taken. I put my mouth close to his ear.

"Thank you for the present, Brock. The diary is beautiful — it's perfect."

With his hands still on my waist, Brock pulled back and looked at me with a puzzled expression.

"Delia — what in the world are you talking about?"

Chapter 6

"Hey, what took you so long to get here?" Jewel asked as I slid into the seat next to her, moments after the bell. Brock ambled to the back of the room where he could sprawl out, and was less likely to have to answer questions.

"I'll tell you later," I whispered.

"What are you whispering for, Delia? The teacher isn't even here yet. Come on, tell me what happened," Jewel prompted, eyes so wide with curiosity they practically had big question marks in them.

"Okay," I answered. "Remember the dream I told you about? Reading the diary?"

Jewel nodded with rapt attention.

I took the diary out of my bag and held it up. "Well, look what I found in my locker, tied with a ribbon."

Jewel's mouth opened wide. Then she

smiled and shook her head. "Wow. What a weird coincidence. Where'd it come from?"

As I started to speak, I noticed that Brenda Ann, who sat in the seat just in front of Jewel, was sitting very still. Jewel followed the direction of my gaze. Then she looked back at me and tilted her head to one side. The unspoken question was, "Is it okay if she hears this?"

I shrugged, silently answering that it didn't matter.

"Hey, Bambi . . . *I mean, Bandy,* if you're going to listen in you may as well turn around."

I winced at Jewel's use of "Bambi" but Brenda Ann ignored the dig. "Why, listen to *what?*" she said, wide-eyed, as she turned to face us. I showed her the diary before I continued with my story, my voice hushed.

"I thought it was a present from Brock. After I recovered from the shock of seeing it, I remembered it was our six-month anniversary. But Brock said he didn't know anything about it."

Jewel tapped her pen on her desk and looked at me, one corner of her mouth curled down. "Is that what he says, eh? Well, my guess is that Mr. Brock has finally decided to play a little joke on you. You forgot about the anniversary, didn't you? So he's decided to play a little prank and tell you he doesn't know where the gift came from."

"I thought of that myself. I don't mind it if Brock and his friends like to play pranks on each other . . . . but I don't want him to start with me."

"Oh, come on, Delia. It isn't like he's starting to play a bunch of goofs on you. It's just a little joke." Jewel shrugged her shoulders. "Don't be so hard on him," she added.

You don't have to stick up for him, I thought. I could feel little pinpricks of irritation beginning to form behind my eyes.

Brenda Ann spoke up. "You probably don't realize it, Delia, but a lot of girls would like to get their hands on Brock Davidson. Plenty tried, and then quiet little Delia waltzes off with him — without lifting a finger."

Brenda Ann looked at me intently. "If you thought Brock was playing a joke on you, the two of you might have a fight. Maybe somebody who's jealous played a prank of their own to cause trouble between you and Brock." She cast a meaningful glance at Jewel.

"Oh, come on. Are you serious?" Jewel looked disgusted.

"Well, *somebody* might do it," Brenda Ann said, defiantly.

"That's pretty farfetched," Jewel grimaced. "Unless *you* did it, Brenda Ann."

"You guys please cut it out. It's not nice." This teasing banter was making me uncomfortable.

"Okay, okay, we'll stop," Jewel said with a little shake of her head. "Anyhow," she continued, "If you want to drive Brock, or whoever did it, crazy — I bet I know a game you can play."

"Playing games" didn't sound like fun. "I don't think I'm really up for it, but try me. What is it?"

"Delia, what they probably expect you to do is to start wondering and racking your brains. Did Brock do it? If not, who did?"

"And I am. So?"

Jewel sighed and rolled her eyes, as if I was being deliberately dense.

"Well, don't say one more word about the diary to Brock or anyone else. Let them wonder if you just forgot about the whole incident. Let them stew for a while."

Mr. Parrish, the English teacher, finally entered. Every once in a while, I felt like I had a crush on Mr. Parrish — actually, just *almost a crush*. Of course, Mr. Parrish was too old for me. His longish, sand-colored hair showed traces of gray at the temples. But I still thought his pale, ice-blue eyes were gorgeous.

"All right, everyone, let's get started."

So Jewel and I had to stop talking.

Even though I knew I was doing just what the prankster would want me to do, I couldn't help it. I couldn't stop wracking my brain, wondering if Brock didn't do it, who did?

Lots of kids exchanged locker combinations. I had Jewel's, and Brock's, and they had mine. But the truth was that the culprit could be almost anyone. The lockers weren't hard to break into, if someone was determined.

But why?

Finally, I was worn out, and stopped trying to analyze the situation.

I gazed at the diary.

Suddenly I was struck by a thought so obvious that I couldn't believe it hadn't occurred to me before. *There might be writing in the diary. After all, it wasn't new.*

I took my notebook and opened it in front of me, and held my pen in my right hand so that it would look as if I were poised and ready to take notes.

I held the diary in my lap.

Now I realized that there was no key for its lock. But I needn't have worried. The little clasp opened easily, even though my hands were trembling. Suddenly it seemed very important to find words on those pages.

For a moment I prayed silently. And then . . .

I knew it.

There was writing in there, all right.

I'm going to be able to read someone else's diary.

Chapter 7

I'm going to be able to read someone else's diary.
I repeated to myself.

The very idea sent a guilty shiver of anticipation down my spine that was so strong I looked around to see if anyone had read my mind. But the rest of the class was absorbed in listening to Mr. Parrish.

Normally, I was an attentive student, *and such a good girl,* that I would have been paying attention, too.

But not today.

Today I had something that was *more* interesting to do.

For an instant I felt that what I was planning to do was wrong — but only for an instant. After all — it wasn't as if I *knew* this girl.

I had already assumed it was a girl, since boys don't usually keep diaries. From the look of this one, it was several years old.

Probably as old as I was.

The girl who had owned it probably was grown up now. She might even have children of her own. Most likely, she'd forgotten all about this diary.

She'd never know about someone else reading it, anyway.

And so I began reading, and let myself be swept into the world between the pages of the diary. Into the world of a girl I was just beginning to know.

The girl who had written in the diary sounded as if she never had a worry in the world, or a single moment of self-doubt. She thought a lot about the way she looked, and boys, and clothes.

She didn't have to be careful and polite, the way I did.

This girl was kind of wild. *She* really knew how to have fun, and *she* wasn't afraid to break a few rules to do it. And she liked to play little jokes on her friends — sort of like the pranks Brock played. The only thing she seemed halfway serious about was art . . . especially painting.

Reading the diary made me feel like I was getting to know the girl who wrote it very well. It was as if she were speaking the words right inside my head, telling me all about herself.

And even though she was different from me, I felt that I understood her.

I only wished that I knew what the initials "LL" stood for. If I knew her name, it would make the diary writer more real — as if I knew her. As if we were friends.

The idea came to me that her name could be anything I wanted it to be — so long as it started with "L," of course! And what a perfect coincidence. My favorite name started with an "L." *Laura.* When I was a child, and we played games, my "pretend" name was always Laura. And so I decided that Laura would be the name for the girl who wrote the diary.

Ordinarily, I probably would have thought "Laura's" pranks weren't funny, or perhaps that her sense of humor was a little mean. Now, however, I began to see things differently. Maybe I had been taking life too seriously. No wonder I didn't have as much fun as Laura did.

In fact — in the midst of all the pressure I was feeling, I envied this girl. She wouldn't let a thing like having to pick a college, or leave a small town, bother her. I wished I could be more like her.

When I finally glanced up from the diary to look at the clock, class was almost over. I couldn't help smiling to myself as I thought about the page I had just finished. The writer had sounded so excited about a new haircut, and the red shoes she'd bought for the prom.

After class, I started to tell Jewel about reading the diary, but something stopped me.

The writing was my secret, and I realized I wanted it to remain that way. There was something thrilling about being the only one to know. There was something a little scary, a little naughty, too.

After all . . . you were never, never supposed to read someone else's diary.

Chapter 8

In the days that followed, I spent all my spare
time reading the diary. I took it with me everywhere I went. I read a page or two in the
morning, and another page or so before I went
to sleep at night. In between, I read in class
when I thought no one was looking — and
every other chance I got.

I would have finished right away, except for
the amount of time it took to read each page.
Normally I was a fast reader, but I could only
get through a little of the diary at a time. While
I was reading, I lost all sense of time. When
I was able to tear myself away, I was always
amazed to find that hours had passed, and I
had only gone through a few pages.

Perhaps it was because I was absorbing
every bit of what I read, getting to know the
girl I called Laura in a way I'd never known
anyone else. I had never known anyone who

was as devoted to keeping a diary as I was, until I read Laura's. She wrote about her feelings and experiences in such detail.

Of course, I'd never read anyone else's diary. It became a link between us. We were bonded by our mutual interest.

Aunt Gracie sniffed with disapproval and adjusted her hairnet whenever I retired to my room after dinner to read. But since I'd started the diary, Aunt Gracie didn't scare me anymore. I knew Laura wouldn't have been afraid of her.

I knew, because I had discovered that Laura and I had a similar problem. Whereas I lived with a mean old aunt, Laura lived with a mean old grandmother. She mentioned the grandmother a lot in her diary. She also mentioned lots of boyfriends, but especially one named Charlie. And she mentioned a cousin her own age who sometimes came to visit the grandmother. Laura called her "Goody-Two-Shoes."

Laura often felt her grandmother treated her unfairly. But she got even, in her own way. When she was angry about something her grandmother did, she'd just make something awful happen to her in her diary. Like the part she wrote when her grandmother made her rake the yard:

There I was, bored to tears from raking leaves, while Grandma and Goody-Two-Shoes sat inside watching TV, and gabbing. Blah, blah, blah. That cousin of mine. As if there was nothing better to do than sit around with Grandma.

Besides, it's too early to rake the yard anyway. A lot more leaves will fall. And there are some deep holes in this yard. Something tells me they're going to get deeper. When the leaves fall, Grandma will never be able to see the holes. What if she steps in one and has an accident? UH-OH!

Reading things like that made me uncomfortable. But I reasoned that Laura was just writing them as a way to blow off steam. She wasn't serious.

The more I read, the more I sensed that there was something that I should find in the diary. Some kind of message, just for me.

Reading the diary began to improve my mood. I found I didn't worry so much. The carefree attitude of the writer, Laura, was catching. She did so many things that were fun.

Why couldn't I try some of the same things? I asked myself.

And so, I did.

A few days after I found the diary, I decided

to do something I'd never done before. Something *daring*.

So I cut class.

It was something Laura did often.

It was easier than I thought it would be.

I headed out a side door, and just started walking. It filled me with such a spirit of adventure that I felt giddy. How could I have stayed shut up in a stuffy old classroom on such a beautiful day?

It felt so wonderful just to be *alive*, I loved the feeling of the sun on my face, and the smell of the air.

And knowing I was doing something *against the rules*.

Just like Laura.

Chapter 9

I just kept on walking, without any plan —
walking and daydreaming about nothing in
particular.

The feeling was exhilarating. Soon I wasn't
walking anymore; I was running. I ran and ran
until I was out of breath and couldn't run anymore.

That's when I realized I was lost.

I didn't think it was possible to get lost in
Pleasantville — but now I was. I found myself
in an old section of town that I wasn't familiar
with. All the houses had wide front porches
and big front yards.

It was quiet, too.

Very, very quiet.

I stood as motionless as possible and lis-
tened. There was no noise of radios or television sets. No children ran shrieking as they
played. No cars whizzed by.

Not a soul was around. The only sound was the faint rustling of the leaves on the trees.

I started to get the feeling I was in one of those TV stories about someone who finds out they're the only survivor on the planet.

And that's when I saw the sign . . . YARD SALE. It hung from a mailbox, swaying slightly in the breeze. It was stuck there with pieces of faded masking tape.

The mailbox stood in front of a dark green frame house. There was a weeping willow tree in the front yard. Whoever lived there wasn't too concerned with keeping the lawn mowed. The yard was overgrown and full of weeds.

I loved to shop at yard sales. But it looked like I was too late for this one. I could see that there was another sign advertising the yard sale on the front porch. Maybe there was some stuff left to sell, inside the house.

I walked past the sign on the mailbox and headed up the walkway. As I started up the steps I had one of those feelings Jewel told me was called déjà vu. *I've been here before.*

For just a fleeting instant, in my mind's eye I could see the house as it might have been once . . . the paint fresh, and the lawn mowed. And for a moment I could imagine running inside, up the stairs to a room in a

43

corner of the house. I would sit in the room . . . and write in my diary.

I tried to peer in one of the windows, but couldn't see anything through the smudges and the film of dust.

"You're wasting your time," I heard a voice say behind me. "There's nobody there anymore."

I turned to see an old man wearing overalls. Why hadn't I heard him come up behind me?

"The place is all closed up. I ought to know — I live right next door."

The man smiled at me . . . and fixed me with the stare of one filmy blue eye. I told myself that he was only an old man, but he scared me. It was because he reminded me of someone.

Who?

Then I remembered. *The boogeyman.* In childhood nightmares, the boogeyman is always hiding somewhere, waiting to find you . . . waiting to kill you.

This old man made me scared the same way — the kind of scared I felt in childhood; the kind of scared that's deep inside, where my worst fears were hiding.

"That's too bad. But I guess they've already had the yard sale, then. The sign looks like it's been here a while." I started backing away.

"Yeah." The man chuckled, revealing an almost menacing-looking row of teeth. "The old lady had the sale after her granddaughter died. Then she moved away to a retirement community. Wasn't much of a yard sale, though. She only had one customer." The man chuckled again, in a thin, high wail. It sounded like a comb being scraped against a blackboard.

"Well, I guess that's that." I stepped toward the edge of the porch, then down one step, then another. As I started up the walkway, the man started after me. "There's no need to leave so soon," he said.

"No . . . no. I've really got to leave. There are people waiting for me." I continued walking, though I wanted to run. So I walked as fast as I dared, trying to seem as if I really wasn't in a hurry.

"Hey — wait!" he called. "I've got to tell you something." Now I heard his footsteps. He was coming after me.

The awful man put his hand on my arm. *His touch felt . . . reptilian.* Then he stared into my face with his filmy blue eye. "There was only one customer at that yard sale. It was a girl. She looked a lot like you. Come to think of it . . . you look a lot like the girl who used to live here. The one who's dead." The word *dead* sounded like a rusty door hinge.

"I've never been here before," I said, becoming more afraid. I wished he would take his hand off my arm. When he didn't, I twisted free.

"I think you have," the man said. "I think you're the one who bought that book at the yard sale." As I backed away he continued to follow me, step for step.

"Don't you want to know how the granddaughter died?" The boogeyman smiled . . . an eerie, smug smile . . . a smile that told me it would make me ask what happened even though I didn't want to know.

I took a deep breath. "What happened?"

"She was murdered . . . by one of her friends."

Chapter 10

I will never know how I managed to get away from the awful man with the filmy blue eye . . . or what happened between the time I left him and found myself in downtown Pleasantville. I only know that the next thing I remember was standing in front of Rose's Doorway to Beauty Salon on Main Street.

I'd never been to a haircutting salon before. My waist-length hair was easy to cut straight across the bottom — so I did it myself.

I was surprised to find myself reaching for the door handle. There were plenty of other places I could have gone. Plenty of other things I could have done with my time. And yet here I was.

The bells over the Doorway to Beauty tinkled as I opened the door.

"Well, hiya, hon," a woman greeted me.

"I'm Rose, and you've just stepped into my Doorway to Beauty."

I'd met Rose before, but I guess she didn't remember me. Today she was wearing a short-sleeved black shirt and cutoff dungaree shorts. Huge hoop earrings dangled from her ears.

Rose didn't look "very Pleasantville," but neither did her salon. The walls were covered with paper in a paisley design, and in between were mirrors and huge posters of models with various hairstyles and pictures from rock concerts.

"What can I do for you?"

Apparently Rose had perfected the ability of being able to speak clearly through a mouth of bobby pins or roller fasteners.

"I'd like — a haircut."

Rose glanced at me as if giving an appraisal. Her eyes were heavily ringed with black mascara, giving her the appearance of a startled raccoon.

"Weren't you in my Doorway to Beauty class I gave over at the high school the first part of the year? The one on Wednesday nights?"

"Well, yes." I felt suddenly shy. "I'm surprised you remember me. I guess I haven't gotten around to putting some of those items on your 'glamour checklist' into practice. My girlfriend kind of dragged me along." I could feel myself blushing.

"It's never too late to glamorize, dear," said a voice. I turned around and I recognized Miss Tilley, who owned Candy 'n Things. My name is *Miss Tilley,* not *Ms.* Tilley, and not *Tilley,* she always told us.

Curlers and curl papers stood out all over Miss Tilley's head, sticking out over her chubby face. She looks like a porcupine covered with candy wrappers, I thought with surprise.

Rose smiled. "It's true that it's never too late to *glamorize.* Have a seat over there while I finish Miss Tilley's permanent wave."

I nodded to Miss Tilley and took a seat.

It looked like Miss Tilley was going to take a while to glamorize. I picked up a magazine and started thumbing through it, but then I remembered the diary. I pulled it out of my bag and continued reading. Laura was talking about getting a manicure.

As I was reading I remembered my own stubby nails had never been polished. *Maybe I'd get a manicure, too.*

I turned a page of the diary.

Now I read that Laura was angry at a girl at school — a rival for some boy's attention. It seemed kind of silly to me, since Laura had so many boyfriends. But angry she was. And, as she usually did when she was angry, Laura thought up a disastrous fate for her enemy, and carried it out in the pages of her diary.

Apparently the girl whom Laura was mad at had a bee farm at the edge of the property where she lived. . . .

I got so furious when I saw her batting her eyes and flirting, talking a mile a minute. Blah, blah, blah. Then I started wondering.

Would it be easy to stir the bees up one day as she walked by? What if a hive fell on her? Imagine, being stung to death. OUCH! What a honey of a way to die.

I found a smile forming on my lips in spite of myself as I read the last words. *A honey of a way to die.* Even when Laura was angry, she had a sense of humor.

I glanced up from the diary to see how Rose was coming along. She was just finishing the last curl on Miss Tilley's head.

When Jewel and I were children, Miss Tilley didn't like it when we came into her store. We didn't do anything wrong, but she always accused us of coming in to steal something.

Every town has its eccentric, and Miss Tilley belonged to Pleasantville. I didn't mind her anymore. She was just an odd older lady. Besides, now that I wasn't a kid, Miss Tilley didn't treat me like one. She probably didn't even remember being mean.

I watched as Rose started squeezing the plastic bottle in her hand, squeezing the permanent wave solution onto Miss Tilley's head.

But something was terribly wrong. As the solution touched Miss Tilley's curls, a wisp of smoke rose up. I heard a faint sizzle, and Miss Tilley let out an agonizing shriek.

What I saw was so awful that I was powerless to move. The salon owner didn't stop to see what was wrong. She just kept squeezing on the solution, in spite of Miss Tilley's horrible cries.

Was Rose crazy . . . or had she made some horrible mistake? What she was squeezing onto the curls wasn't permanent wave solution, it was *acid*.

I was unable to make a sound.

The acid was running over Miss Tilley's head, carving out gulleys and burning deep holes everywhere it touched.

Miss Tilley was screaming, but still Rose kept squeezing on the solution.

Was it possible that I heard what I did? Rose told Miss Tilley to . . . *"Relax, you're going to look very glamorous."*

And then Miss Tilley stopped screaming. Why?

Rose turned the chair around, so that Miss Tilley was facing me.

The acid had eaten a huge hole in Miss Tilley's face.

Miss Tilley was dead.

Well, I thought. It looks like Rose didn't just give Miss Tilley a permanent wave. She gave her a permanent wave . . . good-bye.

"I'm so glad I finally decided to get a permanent wave," Miss Tilley said. "No more going to sleep on rollers."

I blinked.

There was Miss Tilley, as fine as ever. In fact, she turned and smiled at me.

She didn't suspect the horrible death I had just imagined for her.

I felt confused. It was only a *mean thought,* but it was not the kind of thought I was used to having.

It was as if I had seen through someone else's eyes. Through someone else's mind. Even someone else's sense of humor.

It wasn't cold inside the salon, but I looked down and saw chill bumps on my arms.

I knew well who had thoughts like the ones I had just had.

Laura.

In the diary.

Chapter 11

"Delia — we're ready to start now, hon," Rose called. From the tone of her voice I could tell it wasn't the first time she had called me. I leaped to my feet — and then I hesitated. There was still time to change my mind and walk out the door.

That was what I really wanted to do.

But I didn't.

Instead, I allowed myself one more look at Miss Tilley, as if to reassure myself that she really was fine. She smiled back at me. You see? There's no harm in a nasty thought, I told myself. Maybe I'd even write it in my diary, the way Laura did.

Then, Rose and I got started.

First, I got a manicure. That part was easy. I chose a shade called Scarlet Memories. Jewel is going to flip, I thought, as I watched Rose polish my nails.

"You're going to have to come back here to keep these nails looking nice," Rose told me. "Don't ever let me see them looking the way they did when you came in here!"

It was more difficult to sit still as my hair was scissored. At first I was nervous, but Rose was so easy to talk to I soon began to relax.

"You're starting to get some color back in your face, kiddo!" she told me. "When you first walked in here, you looked like a ghost!"

Comb. Pull. Snip.

Hair was falling all over the floor around me.

"Well — I got lost on the way over here. It was scary. I didn't think it was possible to get lost if you'd lived in Pleasantville all your life."

Rose chuckled. "I guess I'd have to agree with you there."

Snip snip.

"Yeah, it was weird. It was this section of town with really big houses. Big front porches. It was really quiet there, too. Nobody around."

"Hmm," Rose said, clipping off a section of hair. "Real huge houses, huh? You don't remember the street, do you?"

I fiddled with the black plastic cape that was tied around my neck to protect my clothes. "You know — I think I saw a street sign, but

I just can't remember. I think you could see some water towers, off behind the houses — and — oh, yes! Every house had a weeping willow tree — at least one — in the front yard."

Rose started cutting another section of hair. "That's funny. I can't think what you mean. They tore down some houses like that — oh — years ago. That's right where the mini-mall is. You know how you can see water towers from the mini-mall?"

She was right. I must have gotten the place confused with someplace else.

When Rose finally said, "Finished!" I was surprised to find that nearly two hours had gone by since I'd walked into the salon.

I had been facing away from the mirror while most of the cutting was done. That's what I had asked for, because I didn't think I could stand watching. Now I found myself simultaneously eager to see the results, and consumed with dread.

What if I looked awful?

I squeezed my eyes shut as Rose spun the chair around to face the mirror. As I opened my eyes, the face that I saw almost took my breath away. The face in the mirror was mine, and yet so different that I had to get used to it. Instead of straight hair that hung on either side of my face, I had wispy bangs and my hair had been cut so that it curled just a little and fell softly over my shoulders.

Rose walked a few steps away, then turned around and looked at me. She shook her head.

"You know, I've got to admit . . . you don't look half bad. In fact, you look good — real good." I could see her smiling in the mirror.

"Like it?" she asked.

"You bet I do."

I swung myself around to face Rose. "I can't believe it. It's incredible. Thanks."

"Your friends are going to like it, too."

Friends. The word made me remember something.

"You know . . . I remember something else that happened when I was lost."

"What?"

"Well — a man told me that a girl who lived in one of the houses was murdered. By one of her friends."

Rose turned pale. "What a terrible thing to say. Don't pay any attention. He obviously was crazy."

I was puzzled. "I was afraid of him . . . and I thought he was weird. But what makes you say he must be crazy?"

"Well, obviously, anyone who told you that

one of your friends was going to kill you is out of his mind."

"That's not what I said. I said he told me that the girl who lived in the house was murdered by one of *her* friends."

Rose looked a little relieved. "Thank goodness. It was giving me chills. I could have sworn you said he told you that *you'd be murdered by one of your friends.*"

Chapter 12

As I left the salon, I hardly felt the sidewalk under my feet because it felt as if I was walking on air.

I couldn't resist checking out my reflection in store windows.

I not only looked different.

I felt like a different person.

But then my mood changed. One minute I was walking on air, and the next minute my euphoria faded. Moment by moment I grew more queasy. *This style isn't me,* I said to myself.

I looked down at my red nails. Even my hands didn't seem like mine.

Aunt Gracie was going to have a fit. What in the world had made me do such a thing? Why, oh, why had I done it?

I could feel myself starting to panic.

By the time I reached home, I was in tears.

As I stood outside, I could hear the phone ringing.

Aunt Gracie didn't like telephones. I knew she would just sit there and let it ring. I fumbled for my keys. Pushing open the door, I ran to the phone.

But by the time I got to it, the caller had hung up.

The house was dark.

Where was Aunt Gracie, anyway?

Slowly, I walked into the kitchen. Ruby, the cat, startled me as she brushed against my legs.

"Poor thing, you must be hungry," I said, soothingly.

Ruby was practically the only object of Aunt Gracie's affection. It was odd that she wouldn't feed her, I thought, as I dumped some cat food in her dish. She gobbled at it greedily.

Then I saw the note from Aunt Gracie, taped to the refrigerator door. It said that a friend of Aunt Gracie's had gone on vacation, and Aunt Gracie was going to stay at her place and take care of the cats and the plants.

I was a little surprised. I'd never heard Aunt Gracie mention a friend, but I was too happy that Aunt Gracie would be away to question it.

I wouldn't have to explain my hair and my

nails . . . at least for a while. There was no one to tell me what to do. Even better, no one to tell me what *not* to do. No one there to make little disapproving sniffs and cast dark glances.

I can even have whatever I feel like having for dinner, I said to myself, grinning at how elated it made me feel. I hoped there was something worth eating in the refrigerator.

"Oh, no," I mumbled as I saw a big bowl of tuna salad. I didn't want that. I hoped there was some leftover macaroni . . . or meat loaf — anything.

Then I had an idea. The girl in the diary *liked* tuna salad. I knew because I had read it when she wrote about a picnic she'd gone to. It struck me that I'd hit upon a good game — to try everything the girl in the diary tried . . . do whatever she did.

"Terrific" I muttered as I took the tuna salad out of the refrigerator and started making a sandwich. Then I took a soda out of the fridge, too. (I usually drank juice or water, but it was soda for me tonight. *She* drank soda.)

A bit apprehensively I took a bite of the tuna sandwich. It was *delicious*. Why had I avoided it at first? I took another bite.

I took the sandwich into the dining room. I made a face at some college catalogs that were on the dining room table as I pushed them aside and sat down.

I ate hurriedly, so that I could get back to reading the diary. Just as I finished the sandwich, I noticed a large paper bag on the floor in the hallway. I must have dropped it when I ran for the phone.

As I examined the contents of the bag, I began to remember where I'd spent some of my time between leaving that strange house and arriving at the haircutting salon.

I'd been shopping.

In the bag was a new unpainted art canvas and some oil paints . . . and a pair of red shoes.

In my haste to answer the phone, I'd forgotten all about the things. I stashed the bag in the corner. I decided to put the canvas and the shoes away later, after I'd read some more of the diary. I fished it out of my purse, and sat down on the couch to read.

I soon learned that Laura always got a manicure before she had her haircut, the same as I had just done. It pleased me to know that.

But as I read further, my heart began to sink.

My haircut was all wrong. Hers was cut "shockingly short." Mine was way too long.

I could feel myself panicking, in spite of the

fact that I knew it didn't make any sense. Moment by moment, I grew more and more upset.

The only way I could calm down was by telling myself that I'd simply have to get my hair cut again tomorrow, the way Laura described her haircut in the diary.

Chapter 13

"You're kidding!" Jewel nearly snorted her "Coconut Hula Surprise" out her nose as she gasped in amazement. "*Another* haircut? You haven't changed your hair one time since I've known you, and now you just had a haircut and you're changing it *again?* Why, Delia? It looks great."

I looked at the Bonzo's Happy Clown and squirmed.

"Thanks, but it's just not . . . right," I said, fingering a strand of hair. "It's just so . . . blah. *Blah, blah, blah.* It's too . . . long. And I want something that stands out, that's not so plain. What I mean is that I want something *flashier.* Something that I feel is — you know — *more me.* A style that . . ." I stopped talking because of the strange look I saw on Jewel's face.

"I've never heard you talk about your appearance so much, Delia. In fact — you hardly ever talk about it. You know — you've been a little different, the past couple of days. Not that I'm criticizing," she said a bit too hurriedly. "It's just . . . different."

"Well, not different enough if you ask me. I've got to get some new clothes. I looked at the contents of my closet last night and practically had a tantrum!"

Jewel shrugged. "I always thought you looked nice."

I looked at my watch. "Jewel, I've got to get going. I want to see if Rose can fit me in today."

Jewel smiled at me. "Okay. I can't believe this, but good luck."

"Good heavens, Delia — back so soon?"

Rose looked up from her magazine, *Secret Confessions,* as I walked into the Doorway to Beauty. "What's the matter, hon? Is there something wrong with your haircut?"

She looked at me with an expression of deep concern, almost as if she were a doctor asking "Where does it hurt?"

"No . . . it's not that there's anything *wrong* . . . exactly."

Rose peered at me.

"It's just that . . . I guess now that I had

the nerve to get my hair cut, I've decided to go short. And I think I'd like it a little lighter."

I had the feeling when I read the diary that Laura's hair was lighter, but I wasn't sure of the color. After trying and trying to figure it out, I hated to think I might be wrong.

Rose looked at me sharply. "Are you sure?" she asked.

I nodded. "Yes. SHOCKINGLY short," I said, borrowing an expression from the diary.

And when I left, it was.

I felt so . . . new. The breeze blew the fringe of bangs off my forehead. All the way home I felt so light, so free.

At home, the house was dark again. I checked the answering machine . . . but Aunt Gracie hadn't left a message. I wasn't worried — Aunt Gracie didn't like using the answering machine. It had taken me months of wheedling and cajoling to get one. Well, I didn't miss Aunt Gracie yet, anyway.

She's one mean old battleaxe, I thought, shocking myself. I chuckled a little, feeling almost daring. I'd always chided myself for such thoughts.

"She's one mean old battleaxe," I said aloud. Then I said it again, louder, defiantly. It felt kind of good. Aunt Gracie *was* mean. Why *should* I try to be so understanding?

I turned on the hall light and stood in front of the mirror. I liked this look. The fact that my hair was finally "right" made me feel confident — upbeat.

And I wasn't worried anymore that I'd gotten a second haircut just because I'd read about a style in Laura's diary. Now I realized that I'd panicked because I wanted to look my best — the way lots of girls do. The other haircut wasn't right — cutting it again was really *my* idea.

As I headed for the kitchen I passed by the clock and realized it was almost time for my favorite show, *Beyond Reason*. *Beyond Reason* was a new weekly TV show that talked about phenomena such as clairvoyance, ESP, psychics, and other such "eerie weirdie" topics. It had developed quite a following among high school students. All my friends made a point of watching it.

Standing in the kitchen, trying to decide what to do about dinner, I realized that I hadn't heard from Ruby, the cat, since I'd been home. Where was that cat, anyway? Funny that she wasn't rubbing around my legs, meowing for something to eat. Well, she was probably off somewhere sleeping.

I remembered how much I had enjoyed the tunafish sandwich the night before, and decided to make one for dinner tonight, too. It would be fun to sit in front of the TV set and eat. Aunt Gracie never let me do that.

I could do without having to sit through another one of our dreary little dinners with her yakking through it.

Before I settled down, I turned off all the lights so that the room was bathed in the glow from the TV screen. It was the perfect atmosphere for watching *Beyond Reason* — it made it seem spookier.

Soon I was sitting comfortably on the couch and munching on my sandwich as I waited for the show to start. I didn't have to wait long.

"Welcome to *Beyond Reason*." The announcer's voice was a mysterious whisper behind the roll of the opening credits. "And now your host, Anton Crystal." He pronounced the name Crisss-TAL, with the accent on the last syllable. I suppose it sounded more exotic than just plain Mr. Crystal.

A small, dark man with hooded eyes that burned like candle flames stared into the camera.

"Hello, I am Crystal, your host of *Beyond Reason* — the show that reminds us that to understand many things in the universe we have to look . . . (a dramatic pause) BEYOND REASON!"

Crystal's voice thundered as he uttered the last words. After another dramatic pause, he continued.

"Tonight, we are going to examine the question of the existence of past lives, and meet some guests who have learned about their own past lives and are here to tell us all about them."

Crystal looked right into the camera, and right out at us, *the folks in television land*. Crystal often did that, looking so intensely hypnotic I almost suspected that one day he would pull out a pocket watch and ask everyone to follow its motion until their eyes got heavy.

Crystal introduced the first guest, Sherry Madsen, a round-faced woman of about twenty-five, with chin-length blonde hair in a conservative page-boy style, and innocent blue eyes. "I was a snake charmer in Barnum and Bailey's circus at the beginning of the twentieth century," she said, solemnly.

Crystal introduced his next guest. She looked the same age as I was. Cindy Kenyon was a small, fragile-looking girl with huge dark eyes. "In my past lives," said Cindy, "I know that I lived as both an Egyptian princess, and a singer in nineteenth-century Spain." Cindy paused and put a hand to her temples for a moment. Then she seemed to stare at something far off in the distance. "I realized that I was an Egyptian princess first, when I saw a picture of myself in a museum."

Next, an elderly gentleman appeared. His eyes were magnified behind the thick lenses of his glasses, making him look owlish. He had the sweet, kindly expression of pictures of grandfathers in children's first-grade readers. "I'm Corbett Watson, and I was Napoléon," he said.

There was a commercial break for a word from their sponsor, the Egress Funeral Home. "You'll rest easy when you plan ahead. In fact, you'll rest in peace."

I had to admit the guests tonight sounded kind of strange. When Jewel and I watched this show together, she just laughed at it, and called it "Beyond Rational" or "Beyond Sanity." Sometimes I laughed, too.

But I wasn't going to dismiss the things I saw on the show as impossible, especially past lives. Especially after the strange things that had happened to me lately . . . the nightmare about the diary, and the eerie feelings that seemed like memories.

Sitting there alone, basking in the bluish

glow of the TV screen, I began to wonder: What if you knew who you were in a past life? What then?

As if reading my thoughts, Crystal reappeared on screen and said, "We have much to learn from our past life, or *lives*. We keep repeating them, coming back again and again, until we learn what it is we are supposed to learn. Until we are able to do that, history repeats itself again and again."

Crystal pressed his palms together as he continued. "Oh, we don't have *exactly* the same life. Some things change. We have different looks, different personalities. Often if we are wild and flamboyant in one life, we are quiet and softspoken in the next."

Now there was a close-up, and Crystal stared intently into the camera, and *out at me*. "But still we go on and on, trying to resolve the same issues . . . and meeting the same people again and again in each life . . . until we learn what we have to know."

What is that? I wondered. After Crystal said "Good night," an inner chill grew stronger and stronger. *What if . . . what if . . .*, I repeated silently to myself several times, before I could bring myself to finish the thought.

What if all you knew about your past life . . . *was how you died?*

Chapter 14

The announcer came on after the final commercial. "Tune in to our next show, and in the meantime, keep looking for the answers . . . BEYOND REASON!"

I turned off the television, but then felt uneasy. The house was quiet . . . too quiet.

I remembered that I wanted to read some more of Laura's diary, and hopped off the couch to get it. I thought about putting on some music as I read, and realized that I had no idea what kind of music Laura liked. She hadn't written anything about it that I'd read so far.

I felt disappointed. Even though the music would be out of date by now, I might have liked it anyway.

With the diary in hand, I turned on the lamp next to the couch. I lay down, propping a pillow behind my head, and opened the diary.

I had just started thumbing through the

pages, looking for the place that I'd left off . . . when I put the book aside abruptly.

There was someone else in the house with me.

All my systems went on alert. My heart beat faster.

Thump-thump. Thump-thump.

I wanted to sit up, but I was afraid to move a muscle. I felt like a single, raw nerve.

Whoever was there hadn't announced their presence.

There was no noise, but I knew someone was there.

To remain still became intolerable.

Very, very slowly, I sat up.

Thump-thump. Thump-thump.

Maybe Aunt Gracie had come home. But she wouldn't worry about being quiet. She always began grumbling as soon as she shut the door.

But there had been no opening or shutting of any door.

I sat very still.

In the air-conditioned room, I could feel perspiration beading on my upper lip and dampening the palms of my hands.

I sat very still, afraid even to move.

You've been watching too many movies, I told myself, desperately. Too many scary films where the girl alone in the house baby-sitting, or alone in the dark woods at camp, is a waiting target for the killer.

But then I saw that the door on the sunporch was open . . . ever so slightly . . .

. . . And then I felt the hands on the back of my neck.

Chapter 15

I'm going to die.

I'm going to die.

I heard the sound of my own scream rip through the air.

I whirled around.

"Brock!!!"

The sight of the little half smile on his face sent electric shocks of rage racing through my veins. I didn't think I'd ever been so furious. I had been so terrified I thought my heart would pound right out through my chest, and all because of his schoolboy prank.

But the smug smile on Brock's face changed in an instant into terror, and then to recognition. For a moment I was completely confused. Then I realized that Brock hadn't expected me to look so different, with shorter hair in a different color. The room was dimly

74

lit. He had surprised me . . . but I had surprised him, too.

The whole situation suddenly struck me as so ridiculous that I couldn't help laughing. I tried to imagine what would have happened if Brock had surprised Aunt Gracie. Then I had a sobering thought. What had just happened wasn't a schoolboy prank. *Brock had broken into my house. Not only had he broken into my house, he had hidden there silently in the shadows.*

Now Brock was just staring at me, quietly. I didn't like the look on his face. There was something . . . ominous . . . about it.

"You really scared me, Brock. I wish you'd stop playing those childish games." I couldn't keep the quaver of uncertainty out of my voice as I looked into Brock's eyes. There was no warmth there.

Brock continued to stand there, as if he hadn't heard a word I said, looking at me with an impersonal stare.

"So, what's up?" I said, after a few moments of uncomfortable silence.

"What do you mean, what's up? What's up is that you stood me up. We had arrangements to meet at the library and study, remember?"

"I don't remember any arrangements to

meet at the library." I thought for a moment. "Is this another joke?"

"No, Delia," Brock said after a moment. "It's not a joke at all."

I could feel the tension in the air between us.

Brock walked to the dining room table where the college catalogs were laid out. "If you say you don't remember, you don't remember." He picked up the one for Harrison, *coincidentally the college he was going to*. It happened to be on the top of the pile.

Brock held up the catalog. His frosty expression had thawed a little. "So, I guess you finally chose. You picked Harrison, right?"

I hated the conversation that I knew would be coming.

But I knew I couldn't stop it, either. "I haven't picked where I'm going to go, Brock."

"Well, you know why I want us to go to the same school. I want us to have a future together. It's important to me, Delia."

The authoritative tone in his voice was irritating. "Well, what about what's important to *me*?"

"I thought *being with me* was important to you." Brock's voice was brittle. His jaw was clenched, his deep eyes hard and cold.

"Maybe it's *not* important," Brock went on.

"Maybe that's why you *forgot* to meet me at the library."

My stomach started to churn.

I touched my hair. "Brock, if you think I was with another guy, I wasn't. I was getting my hair cut."

Brock was quiet for a moment. He sat down on the couch.

"I can be a real jerk sometimes." He looked embarrassed. "I'll ease up on the college thing." Brock looked at me for a moment. "You look so different — but I like it. Your new hairstyle, I mean," he added sheepishly.

I was relieved to see that the steely expression was gone. "It sounds like such a big deal when you say . . . *future together*. You mean a lot to me . . . but we're only in high school, Brock."

Brock nodded.

"Hey, what's this?" he asked, picking up the remaining piece of my sandwich from the dish on the tray.

"A tuna fish sandwich?" It was so obvious that I felt silly saying it.

Brock tilted his head to one side.

"Didn't you tell me you were allergic to tuna fish?"

It was true. How could I have forgotten?

But I'd eaten tuna fish for two days in a row,

and nothing bad had happened to me. I thought for a moment. "You know, my aunt *said* I was allergic to it . . . but I don't think I remember ever actually eating any up until now. She must have been wrong."

Brock shrugged. "Congratulations. Listen . . . tomorrow, let's pretend this whole night never happened, okay?"

"Okay."

Brock kissed me lightly on the lips, and left, pulling the door on the sunporch tightly closed.

I stared after him. I wished I hadn't seen the expression in his eyes that I'd seen tonight. For a fleeting instant, I wondered just how angry he could get.

But immediately, I dismissed my fears. Brock wasn't violent, or mean.

He just had a bad temper sometimes.

Chapter 16

With a last look at the red tooling on the cover, I snapped the diary shut, clicking the little clasp as I slid it under my desk. Mr. Parrish had just entered the classroom and put down his briefcase. While I watched him begin shuffling papers I let my thoughts dwell on what I had just read.

Laura had just cheated on a test. Apparently she made a habit of it, as she did of shoplifting and sneaking out at night. Care always had to be taken to prevent her cousin — the one she called "Goody-Two-Shoes" — from finding out. Goody-Two-Shoes was always held up to Laura as an example of fine behavior. But Goody-Two-Shoes was also a tattletale. And an ever-watchful one at that.

Because she was a tattletale, Goody-Two-Shoes didn't get much enjoyment from her virtuous standing. She was constantly the object of Laura's teasing and practical jokes. While I always read of these torments with distaste the first time, invariably they made me smile later on. After all, I reasoned, Laura was just having fun. She didn't mean to cause any harm.

While I had come to accept the teasing and practical jokes, the cheating and shoplifting still made my stomach churn uncomfortably. Those were things I had never done, and reading about Laura doing them was the same as finding out a friend had done something you didn't approve of.

I reached inside the desk and shoved the diary further toward the back. As I did it, a tiny shock ran through me.

Suddenly I imagined Laura ridiculing me. I felt the flush of embarrassment creep into my cheeks.

"Something wrong? Why are you all red?" Jewel asked me as she swung into the seat next to mine.

"Am I?" I shrugged. "Maybe it's hot in here."

"I feel okay. Listen, did you study for the test?"

I squinted as I looked at Jewel. "Are you kidding? What test?"

Before Jewel could answer, a stack of

sheets containing questions was plopped onto the desk in front of me.

"*That* test," Jewel said, pointing. "Where was your mind when Parrish told us about it?

I felt someone poking me in the back. "Pass the questions back," whispered the guy behind me. Mutely I took a sheet of questions and passed the rest of the stack back. I could feel myself start to panic. Now I knew that my face was red, but with a different kind of embarrassment than before. Where, indeed, had my mind been when Mr. Parrish told us about the test?

I probably had been daydreaming . . . *or reading*. My heart started doing flip-flops.

At last I had to admit what I didn't want to. There had been a problem with reading the diary that I had tried to make myself ignore.

In the past few weeks, I'd spent almost no time on homework. I was a good student, and good grades were easy for me. It was near the end of senior year and we didn't have to hand in a lot of homework each day.

Nothing bad had happened . . . yet.

Plus, I knew that my attention in class had been flagging. I often lapsed into daydreaming about things I read in the diary. Of course I always planned for things to change. Day after day I told myself I'd go home to catch up on assignments I'd neglected before doing any diary reading. But — I always changed my mind. I'd pick up the diary, telling myself I was only going to read a few pages.

When I stopped reading I would find that hours had gone by.

Usually I was able to do what I put my mind to. But now I just didn't. Sometimes I didn't even know what happened. I just found the diary in my lap.

Today I promised myself that after this test, I'd pay attention in class. And tonight, I'd go home and study. I really mean it, I told myself.

But unfortunately, I'd have to pass this test first.

"You've all had ample time to prepare, so I don't even need to wish you good luck," the teacher said as he handed out the exam booklets.

Ample time, I echoed in my mind. With a sigh I looked at the list of questions.

When on earth had he talked about these things? I looked frantically around the classroom. No one showed a trace of the panic I felt. Everyone was bent quietly over their papers, pencils moving as they marked off answers.

My mind must have been on a very long vacation. What on earth was I going to do??

And then an idea came to me.

Brenda Ann Bandy had her paper sitting out over the edge of her desk . . . as usual. I had never taken advantage of that fact, and scrupulously avoided letting my gaze stray toward her paper.

It's the wrong thing to do.

But it would be so easy.

Goody-Two-Shoes.

I could see a whole row of answers. I knew Brenda Ann was always right. She'd marked a,b,a,d,e,e. It would be so easy, I said to myself again. And then I'd be able to see another row, and another row. . . .

No. I told myself. I didn't want to do it. I'd do the best I could, but I wasn't going to cheat. I didn't want to do it.

But if I didn't want to do it, why was I looking around to make sure no one was watching me as I gazed at Brenda Ann's paper?

If I didn't want to do it, why was my hand holding my pencil and marking firmly in space after space, *a, b, a, d, e . . .*

Go ahead. Do it.

Of course I can do it. I've done it before.

No.

Oh, it's easy. I've done it before.

The legs of my chair scraped against the linoleum floor as I stood up. I didn't care that everyone had turned to look at me. I could feel a vile taste rising up from my throat, choking me. Nausea threatened to overcome me.

I ran from the room. The sound of my footsteps echoed in the lonely, yawning corridor.

I was barely able to get to the restroom before I was violently sick.

Chapter 17

I didn't go back to class that day. I had to go home and think.

Something very strange and scary was happening to me. I'd been lying to myself for some time now, pretending everything was fine. But I couldn't pretend anymore.

I hadn't wanted to cheat . . . but I almost couldn't stop.

The effort had *actually made me sick*.

Lately I'd been doing more and more things that I'd read in Laura's diary. I knew I was changing . . . but I didn't care. I had never tried to *stop* doing any of the things . . . I'd been having too much fun.

In my mind I went over some of the things that had happened in the past couple of weeks. . . .

There was a barbecue at Brenda Ann Bandy's house. Brock and I danced every dance.

But I never liked to dance before I read about it in Laura's diary.

I had a whole different style lately. I cracked jokes, did unusual things, and made outrageous remarks. I remembered that last week I was with a crowd of my friends at the mall, and I told a woman that I'd seen her car get stolen. I'd only wanted to make my friends laugh. They did, too, when she panicked and ran out.

Later, I realized that the laughter was more from shock than anything else. But I had thought it was very funny at the time. I just wanted to shock people . . . to attract attention.

It was the sort of thing I read about in Laura's diary.

My friends had started commenting on how I'd changed.

Those haircuts I'd gotten, *trying for the same look I'd read about in Laura's diary. I'd even changed the color of my hair.*

The manicures I kept getting. The polish had to be exactly the right color. *The red one I imagined Laura wore.*

I had even stopped writing in my own diary so that I could spend more time reading Laura's.

I was *thinking* like Laura, and *feeling* like Laura, more and more. And more and more, I couldn't even tell the difference. Was it Laura doing the thinking, or me? I was trying to stem the tide of panic that engulfed me, when the ringing of the phone made me jump.

"Hello?"

"Hi, Delia. Aren't you tired of playing games and teasing? Why don't you just be honest?"

"Who are you?"

"You'll find out soon enough."

"You're not funny, you're sick," I said as I slammed the receiver down. If anyone was playing games, it wasn't me.

The phone rang again. Slowly, I lifted the receiver. "Hello?"

For a moment there was no sound.

Then I heard rushing water. "Sound familiar?" the caller asked me in a muffled, faraway voice, and hung up.

When the phone rang a third time, I didn't wait for the caller to speak. "What do you want?" I shrieked into the phone.

"Delia? Is that you?"

It was Jewel's voice.

"Oh, yeah, Jewel. I just had some prank phone calls."

"Don't give the jokester the satisfaction of

getting mad. Anyway, what happened to you in Parrish's class today? I looked for you after class, but I couldn't find you."

"All of a sudden I felt sick. It must have been something I ate. But I'm okay now."

"Then you're going to keep your date with Brock?"

"Huh?" I mumbled.

"You told me you had a date with Brock tonight . . . didn't you?"

I did.

"Yes, I'm keeping my date with Brock. But I've got to hurry and get ready. I'd better go now."

"Okay . . . 'bye."

Brock had been so nice lately. He'd kept his promise, and not said a word about college.

Maybe I could tell him what had been happening to me.

If I could find a way.

I began rummaging through my closet for something to wear. Apparently I'd gotten some new clothes I didn't remember buying.

They were at the very back of my closet.

With the tags still on.

And I knew why. I hadn't bothered to pay for them.

I remembered now. I'd gotten them right after I'd read about shoplifting, in the diary.

For a long time, I stood there, leaning against the wall. I remembered that at first I hadn't wanted to steal those things. But then I had done it quite purposefully. Now I realized that after I read something in the diary, I *had to do it*.

I had no choice.

What had started as a whim, had become an obsession I couldn't control.

Chapter 18

"You look beautiful, Delia." Brock reached across the table and took my hand. "You have a whole different style, lately. You keep surprising me."

I surprise myself, too, I thought.

"What do you think of this place?" Brock asked.

"Oh — it's wonderful." That was the truth. I hadn't expected anything so fancy. "Thank you for a terrific evening."

Brock leaned across the table and stared into my eyes. "It's not over yet."

I could feel my heart beating faster. The way Brock was looking at me made me want to do nothing but sit there just like this, holding his hand and looking into his eyes forever.

"Excuse me. Will that be all?" The waiter was standing by our table.

Brock dropped my hand and we both sat up

straight. I could've killed the waiter. He had no sense of timing.

"Just the check, please," Brock said. The waiter put it down, and walked away.

Brock reached into his jacket pocket. Then he tried another pocket. His eyebrows knitted together in an expression of confusion. I saw him reach first in one pocket of his trousers, then another.

He shrugged.

Then he went through the whole thing again.

"I can't find my wallet," he said finally, looking embarrassed.

I didn't even bother to check my purse. "Oh, no! Brock, what can we do? I only have five dollars. This is awful!"

I stared at the table as I racked my brain for a solution. "I know, we'll just call someone. That's it! I'll just call Jewel."

I looked up to see Brock holding up his wallet, a big grin on his face.

"Gotcha!" he said.

It was just a stupid prank, I thought, disgusted. For a moment I considered telling him just how stupid I thought it was . . . but then I didn't. I didn't want to spoil the evening.

Brock was obviously pleased with himself. "I'm sorry, I know you don't like pranks . . . and I try to hold myself back, but sometimes I just can't stop myself." Brock put several bills on the tray that held the check. "That ought to do it."

I got a tiny bit of satisfaction from the fact that Brock spilled what was left of his soda as he pushed his chair out and started to stand up. The drops were all over his pants.

"Well, I guess I was just punished for my prank," he said, brushing at the droplets. "Just excuse me a minute, while I go clean up."

While Brock was gone I studied the surroundings. Each table had a white tablecloth and a candle burning in a frosted glass holder. Each table also had little roses in a bud vase. It was really elegant.

The waiter hadn't taken the check and the money yet. I looked at the bills on the tray, and I got an idea.

Even as my hand reached and removed two of the bills, I couldn't believe I was doing it. As I saw Brock returning to the table, I slipped the bills in my purse.

"So," said Brock, looking a little damp but otherwise great, "ready to go?" Then he looked at the bills on the tray, puzzled. "The waiter didn't take the check yet . . ."

"No, he came by, but then he just went

away," I said. "Are you sure you left enough money?"

"Oh, sure I did . . ." Brock counted the bills once, then again. "Well, maybe not." He reached into his wallet. Then he counted the bills again. "Oh, no. Delia — you won't believe this."

"You're not going to try the same gag again, are you?" I asked, barely able to suppress a smile.

"No!" Brock shook his head vigorously. "I guess we've got to call someone after all. . . ."

"No, we don't." I couldn't help laughing as I pulled the bills out of my purse. "Look what I found. *Isn't that funny?*"

The expression of surprise and disbelief on Brock's face was truly comical. For a moment he was speechless. He stared at me, his mouth hanging open.

"I can't believe *you* did that!" he said, finally.

I couldn't resist just one smug nod.

As we left the restaurant and headed out into the evening air, Brock's hand was in the middle of my back. Once outside, he put his arm over my shoulders. For a moment we walked in silence.

I loved the feeling of being so close to him. If he had a little problem with pranks, well, hopefully he'd grow out of it. Otherwise, I thought, he's perfect.

"Delia, there's something we've got to talk about."

I was afraid that I knew the conversation that was coming, and I knew I couldn't do anything to stop it.

"You know," Brock whispered in my ear. "I've been true to my word and I haven't said anything . . . but it really would be a big help to me to know that we were going off to college together. It means a lot to me."

I swallowed hard. I wished I could do what Laura would have done. Just lie . . . and then if I wanted to I could simply say I'd changed my mind.

But I couldn't do that. I'd told little fibs to avoid hurting somebody's feelings . . . but I'd never deliberately deceived anyone about something . . . *important.*

I hoped we weren't going to have a fight.

Brock stopped walking and took his arm from around my shoulders.

"Well?"

I could feel the edge in his voice. We *were* going to have a fight . . . unless . . .

Maybe I *could* lie.

Why spoil a perfect evening?

Go ahead. Do it.

And so, I lied.

I told Brock that I'd decided to go to Harrison, the same school he was going to.

It wasn't difficult at all.

Like everything else I read about in Laura's diary, once I tried it, it seemed to come naturally.

Chapter 19

Lying to Brock was simple — at first. But as time went on it got more and more difficult.

Not that lying to him bothered me. Like other things I read about in Laura's diary, it got easier with practice.

It was just that he kept questioning and questioning me about little details.

What was I going to pack to take to school?

Did I remember the date for freshman orientation?

What dorm had I been assigned to?

I finally got so tired of having pretend conversations about college, that one day I just blurted the whole story out. I told Brock I'd lied to avoid having a fight.

Naturally, Brock was pretty angry. His temper flared up in a big way, and things got pretty ugly.

After that we didn't have much to say to each other. When we saw each other at school, we maintained an uneasy truce.

To stop thinking about Brock, and to stay away from reading the diary, I started fooling around with the oil paints and the canvas I'd bought.

Of course, I didn't have much hope that anything would come of it. I never was much good at art class. I liked crafts — making necklaces and things, though. But I hadn't tried drawing since scribbling with crayons in grammar school.

As soon as I started, though, painting seemed familiar. How did I know that the paints were mixed with linseed oil . . . or what the turpentine was for?

But I did.

I just knew how to do it, as if someone had taught me, and suddenly — now I remembered. It was one more thing I had read about in the diary, and made my own. Just like *lying, cheating, stealing,* and the other things I read.

It should have bothered me. But I was so caught up with what I was doing . . . so *enthralled,* that the fear was pushed out of my mind.

As soon as I took the brush in my hand, I

knew what I was going to paint . . . a self-portrait. From the moment I began, I felt that I'd painted many, many pictures.

Hours upon hours passed as I painted. At times I felt myself falling into a trance as I brushed the colors on the canvas. I knew I felt the guidance of an unseen hand. But I told myself that this was what it was to *have a gift* for something.

Day after day, I returned to the picture. I spent every spare minute painting . . . just as at first I'd spent every spare minute reading the diary. I was completely carried away, and probably more than a little crazy. I couldn't believe my skill!

No words could explain the feeling that gripped me when I looked at the finished picture. It was beautiful . . . more than a self-portrait, it seemed to have a life of its own. My work on the picture was through.

And then I put my brush down. *Finished.* I said to myself, suddenly feeling strange. I had spent day after day working on it . . . *consumed by it.*

I looked in the mirror that I'd used while painting the self-portrait. Then I took a long look at the finished product. *The likeness I'd created was . . . astonishing.*

Suddenly I felt overwhelmingly tired. I ran

my fingers through my hair as I turned away from the mirror I'd been looking into as I painted. Fatigue overcame me, penetrating my body as if washing through it like a wave.

I had to sit down on the floor.

For several moments I sat there, feeling faint and dizzy. And then an overwhelming thirst parched my mouth. My lips felt like dry bones and the inside of my mouth like cotton batting.

It was the thirst that brought me to my feet. I lurched over to the sink, desperate for water.

I reached the sink and I turned on the tap and put my mouth to the rushing water, drinking in huge gulps. As I drank I felt my energy returning. What on earth had happened to me? I felt as if I was returning to myself.

I glanced at the mirror I'd used to paint the self-portrait. And then I turned to look at the painting again.

And when I saw it, I gasped. Such a shock of horror ran through me that my knees nearly collapsed.

The likeness I had created was astonishing . . . that's what I remembered thinking when I last looked at the picture.

Now I saw it as if for the first time.

I'd painted the figure as if bathed in an eerie glow. The hair clung close to the scalp, wet, and droplets of water dripped onto the shoulders.

The skin was a clammy, chalky white.

Huge eyes glittered in their sockets and stared out from the canvas beseechingly. The lips had a bluish cast.

Moment by moment some new thing that I saw in the picture became more terrifying than the last.

Now I could see there was something terribly wrong with the portrait that I'd painted.

I had painted a picture of a corpse.

Chapter 20

I turned the painting to the wall and left it in the basement like that, without going near it. I didn't tell anyone about it. I was too terrified.

And then, after a few days, I forgot about the fear. I felt like my old self again. Or did I feel more like *Laura?*

I was walking home from the Doorway to Beauty one evening, annoyed that keeping up my manicure was so difficult now that I was painting, too. Then I saw that a new store had opened up.

I crept closer and read the sign. MADAM RANDA: FORTUNE'S EYE I read. An eye was painted on the sign, surrounded by what looked like sun's rays.

Through the window I saw a woman I presumed was Madam Randa. She was middle-aged, and wore her gray hair parted in the center. There was nothing particularly remarkable about the way Madam Randa looked. That's why the mysterious quality I felt radiating from her was so impossible to explain.

When she saw me looking at her, Madam Randa gazed up at me with a look of recognition. She nodded to me, as if she'd been sitting there waiting for me to arrive.

Stretching out her hand, she motioned for me to come inside. Feeling as if I was already in a hypnotic trance, I did.

The air in the shop was much cooler than the air outside. There was music — soft, like the ripple of silk. On the floor were thick rugs.

Madam Randa began to arrange some jewelry in a glass case. After a few minutes she looked up and said, "You are seeking something. I can feel the aura — the energy around you."

I could only nod.

Madam Randa said nothing more. Her intense dark eyes stared into mine . . . and I found myself talking — telling her everything that had been happening. But even before I finished my story, Madam Randa motioned for me to stop.

"You are having interference from a past life," she said calmly, as a doctor might tell you that you have broken your arm. "To know about a past life is good. To relive it as you are doing can be . . . dangerous. Unless you examine your life, you will keep repeating it until you learn what it is you are supposed to know."

"That's what Crystal said on *Beyond Reason!*"

The moment the words were out of my mouth I knew that I'd made a mistake. At the mention of Crystal, Madam Randa wrinkled her nose in an expression of distaste.

"Crystal is a quack," she said, spitting out the words as if to get rid of the bad taste in her mouth.

In spite of the fact that everything she said seemed to be exactly the same kind of thing I had heard on *Beyond Reason,* I decided it was best not to argue.

"Fake and idiot. Fake and idiot," Madam Randa muttered, pacing up and down. Then, quite suddenly, she calmed herself.

"This Crystal — it doesn't matter. What you need is to have a regression. To return to look at your past life, to see why these things are happening to you."

Strangely enough, I had no hesitation about doing what she suggested. I didn't even flinch when she suggested the price. Aunt Gracie's credit card would take care of that. I'd find a way to pay for it later, I told myself.

At that point I was so desperate, I would have tried almost anything to find out what was going on.

But then, I didn't *really believe* it would work.

Chapter 21

Madam Randa led me to a small room without windows in the back of the shop. There were cushions on the floor.

She instructed me to lie down and placed one of the pillows under my head. The lights were dimmed, and then Madam Randa began to instruct me, in a low, hypnotic chant, to relax. "Your whole body feels as if it is floating, floating on air. Calm and peaceful."

I was dimly aware of the soft music in the background. "You will concentrate only on the sound of my voice." And after a while, indeed, the voice was all I heard. Even the sound of the music was gone.

"Now, imagine you are letting go of your conscious mind . . . as you would let go of a butterfly and let it free. You are letting go of all the thoughts in your conscious mind, and now you are free to let in your memories of your past. You are ready to begin going backward through the tunnel of time. Picture yourself in this long tunnel, and begin the journey backward, backward, backward.

"Do not be afraid of anything you may find in your past. You will be protected by a gentle cushion of light. With this light cushion around you nothing can harm you."

I closed my eyes, and I tried to picture myself in a tunnel. I imagined it was brick all around me, and I walked through the tunnel on a cement path.

But then something miraculous happened. I didn't have to try to picture anything anymore . . . it just happened. The cement and the brick faded, replaced by a tunnel of . . . what . . . light? Air? I couldn't describe it except to say that it was like falling within, and within, and within.

Instead of being surrounded by light, I was heading toward light, rocketing faster and faster and faster. I could no longer hear the sound of Madam Randa's voice.

Just as I wanted to cry out, to stop . . . I did stop. I was motionless, and in the dark.

Where was I?

I suddenly became aware of a noise, somewhere in the distance — but growing nearer and nearer, closing in on me. At first it was the kind of noise you hear when you hold a seashell up to your ear.

But then there were more noises, and they grew louder and louder — and louder! The soft whoosh that sounded like the tide was now like the pounding of the surf roaring in my ears. I not only heard it. I felt it. My head hurt.

In the middle of the surf pounding and roaring I became aware of another sound — that of a kind of bass drum. Its thudding, too, grew louder and louder. *Ga-gung. GA-GUNG. GA-GUNG.*

And then another instrument joined this hideous band. Suddenly there was the deafening noise of castanets — *clickety-clackety. Clickety-clackety. Clickety-clackety.*

Ever so slowly I began to realize that the rushing sound was only the blood pumping through my veins. The thudding, drumlike sound was really a *thump-thump thump-thump*. It was my heart. The clickety-clackety of castanets was really the chattering of my teeth.

As I understood all this, the hammering of my heart began to slow, and I calmed down — at least, a little. For I still felt strange — off-balance, incomplete, somehow.

I summoned every ounce of effort I possessed, and focused it all on lifting my head and looking upward. And then . . . it worked. In fact, after I lifted my head, movement was easy. I found I was able to move my hands, my arms, my legs, and look around.

For an instant, I felt that I was at home . . . in familiar surroundings. I thought I was in my own room. Until I began to take a closer look. . . .

One by one, my vision registered each object — the posters on the walls, the desk, the chair, the lamp, the dresser. My mind began to argue with itself, for somehow I knew the room was *supposed to be mine.*

BUT I DIDN'T RECOGNIZE THESE THINGS.

On the night table was a picture in a frame, of a handsome boy with longish, sand-colored hair and light blue eyes. He looked out from the photograph, lips turned in a gentle half smile. I stared at it for a moment, wondering what the picture was doing there, for I had absolutely no idea who the boy was.

Then I noticed the record albums on the shelf in the corner.

Not CDs . . . records.

And the machine beside it was a turntable.

There was another machine on the desk. It wasn't a computer.

It was a typewriter.

Where was I? *Who was I?*

I ran to the mirror that stood over the dressing table.

And started screaming.

I didn't recognize the reflection in the mirror.

The face wasn't mine.

Chapter 22

Somehow, Madam Randa brought me out of the regression. She had to wait for me to stop screaming before I could tell her what had happened.

"What did the face that you saw in the mirror look like?" she wanted to know.

I let out a sigh so deep I startled myself. "I don't remember. Pretty or plain — old or young — I don't know. All I remember was that it looked like someone . . . dead."

As I held my head in my hands, Madam Randa told me her interpretation of the regression.

When I got up to leave, she asked if I'd be back for "another trip into the past."

I told her I didn't think I could take it.

The house was dark again when I got home. I was starting to get a little worried about Aunt Gracie . . . but then again, I knew she was probably fine, and she'd be very angry if I called the police.

I flung myself on the couch and lay there in the dark, thinking.

If I truly believed that what had happened had been real, then I had seen into my other life somehow. Madam Randa thought that the personality that I had seen in my past life was a very strong one. Something had happened back then that the person I was had sworn to put right in the future.

I remembered the look of horror I had seen on the face in the mirror. What had caused that horror, I wondered. Could it be that I had been — murdered?

I told myself it couldn't be true. But Madam Randa thought it was. She thought that the most logical explanation for all the things I had been experiencing lately was that my old self was trying to contact my new self so that I could remember to avenge my own death.

Madam Randa gave me something else to think about, too. She said that if I knew now that I had a past life, I must realize that other people had them, too. Probably other people that I knew before . . . I knew now.

The thought made me very, very queasy. What if Madam Randa was right . . . I had been murdered? What if my murderer was a teacher . . . or my best friend . . . or Brock? Would I ever know?

Not a pleasant thought.

But . . . was what I had experienced real at all? I couldn't be sure.

There was no sense of having a revelation. The more I thought about it, the more I realized I might have just gotten overly involved with my own imagination.

I finally decided that that's what had happened. There would be no more meetings with Madam Randa.

Thinking that it was crazy to lie there in the dark, and not wanting to feel crazy, I pulled myself off the couch. I started toward the hall to switch on the light.

"OW!" I muttered in surprise as my foot struck a table.

Suddenly, a voice came out of the darkness. "Delia?"

I backed up, looking around wildly for what I couldn't see.

"Aren't you tired of playing games and teasing? You shouldn't have started to play games with me. You should remember that in the end, I always win."

Chapter 23

I took another step backward and stumbled against something.

Something alive.

It rocketed past me with a screeching cry. *"Reeeeowww!"*

By the time my body got the message that fear was unnecessary, and let my hands begin dropping to my sides, my mind already understood. The screeching rocket was the cat.

But whose voice had I heard?

The fear had left me so drained that my legs were weak. I had to lean on the couch for support. The beep of the answering machine confirmed my suspicions.

The cat had somehow pulled the machine cord or stepped on a button or done something to trigger the recording. The voice had come from the answering machine tape.

After the beep, there was another message.

"It's been a long time since we spent some *quality* time together, Delia. I just keep waiting around for you, though. Give me a call. You know who."

I breathed a sigh of relief. I *did* know who that was. It was Brock.

There was another beep.

"Delia, I stopped by earlier, but you weren't there. We're going to study together tonight, remember? I'll come by again, or call you later. This is Jewel. 'Bye."

I was glad to hear that Jewel was coming over. Being alone in the house, except for the cat, gave me the creeps.

Of course, it had been a relief to find that the voice was only on an answering machine, and not coming from someone in the house with me. But after the initial relief, I had to ask myself. How happy could I be about a threatening message on the phone?

Then the phone rang again.

I jumped.

It rang again. And again.

I stood there and stared.

What if it's Jewel?

What if it's Aunt Gracie?

What if it isn't . . . what if it's . . .

The call that I got before was only a prank, I told myself as the phone rang again.

People got them all the time.

It was just a phone call. Nothing more.

Slowly, I lifted the receiver. "Hello?"

For a moment, there was no sound. Then, I heard laughter.

I gripped the receiver tightly. From the static, I knew that what I was hearing was a tape. And not one of very good quality, either.

"Delia, look out the back door. There's a present for you. With a special message."

The caller hung up. Obviously, the tape had been made to disguise the voice. I had no idea who it was.

For a long time I didn't go to the back door.

When I finally did, I was afraid to turn on the porch light.

But finally, I couldn't stop myself, as scared as I was.

And I had a feeling that nothing too terrible was in store for me . . . yet. Whoever had made the tape I'd just heard on the phone was having too much fun scaring me.

i hoped.

That's why when I saw the box tied with a white ribbon and a big bow on the back porch, I decided to open it.

I knew it was a foolish thing to do. But curiosity got the best of me.

I put my ear to the box.

I couldn't hear anything ticking inside.

And so I untied the ribbon . . . and took the top off the box.

The explosion nearly knocked me off my feet.

Chapter 24

BOIIIINGGG!

Well, it wasn't actually an *explosion,* I admitted when I caught my breath. Perhaps it was more the surprise that made me jump.

It was only a jack-in-the-box.

Not a very cheery one.

Whoever had left it for me had quite a sense of humor.

The jack-in-the-box character was a little clown.

The clown was holding a piece of paper with a message.

REMEMBER, DELIA? I'M ALWAYS WATCHING YOU.

The message was written on a page that had been torn from a diary.

The paper was smeared with blood.

And so was the little clown.

On closer examination, I decided that the

"blood" wasn't blood at all, just red paint. It was really just a disgusting prank. I was so angry, I threw the little clown into the backyard.

Half an hour later, when I wasn't so angry, I went back to find it.

But it was gone.

Probably dragged off by the neighbor's dog, I said to myself as I went back inside. I paced the floor and looked at the clock.

I wished Jewel would hurry.

Finally, the doorbell rang.

"Hi," Jewel said in a dispirited voice, as I opened the door. Her hair was disheveled and there was a smudge of dirt on her cheek. Her face wore an expression of disgust. Without saying a word, she slumped through the door and threw herself down on the sofa.

"Are you okay?" I asked, plunking myself down on the couch beside her. Considering what I'd just been through, it seemed a strange question to be asking someone else.

"I'm just in a bad mood," she said irritably. "I slipped on the way over, and all my books and papers went flying. It took forever to pick them up." Jewel examined me with narrowed eyes. "Have you gotten *another* haircut? And some *more* new clothes? You always look like you've just stepped out of a magazine lately."

The edge in her voice startled me.

"Is something wrong with that?"

Jewel sighed and slipped herself off the sofa onto the floor. It was her favorite place to sit. "No — no. I guess not," she said after a moment.

I had been eager to talk to Jewel about my past life regression, and to tell her about the phone calls. But it seemed that she was angry with me about something. Her manner made me hesitate.

"Why don't we go into the den to study," I suggested.

"Okay." Jewel shrugged. She hauled herself off the floor in a tangle of arms and legs, and the jangle of bracelets.

"Did you ever think that maybe, just maybe, it's possible that we all had a past life?" I ventured tentatively as we walked along.

"Oh, come on, Delia. I can't believe you're really taken in by any of that eerie weirdie stuff," Jewel replied, in a voice laden with scorn.

"It's not so weird," I said, hearing how defensive I sounded.

Jewel shook her head. "People who say they've lived before always claim they were generals and princes or movie actresses or something else like that in their former lives. Never anyone ordinary."

"That's not true!" I said emphatically.

"Well, that's all I've ever heard. And another thing. Through the centuries, the population of the world has been increasing. If everyone keeps living over and over again, how come the number of people doesn't stay the same? If everybody lived before, then where do all the new people come from?"

It seemed like Jewel was working up a full head of steam about the topic. "People that believe they're reincarnated and things like that are so *pathetic*. They find ways to fit what are just coincidences into their fantasies. They ought to realize they've got a problem, and they need help."

I hadn't expected her to have such a definite opinion. I decided this conversation better not go any further. For now, anyway.

We reached the den and walked over to the table where I'd piled up the books and other things we'd need to study for the history test.

Jewel glanced down at her hands as she sat down. Then she got up again.

"I'm going to go wash my face," she said.

"Sure," I told her, pulling up a chair. I was sure there was something the matter with

Jewel. I wished she would tell me what it was.

But it seemed that Jewel wasn't going to. She left the room without a word.

I got out the history book and scanned the parts I'd underlined. I started jotting down some possible test questions.

Minutes ticked by.

I jotted down some more questions.

Still Jewel didn't return.

I looked at my watch. It couldn't take her nearly half an hour to get cleaned up a little.

I left the den, and walked toward the bathroom.

The door to the bathroom was open, and there was no light on inside.

I continued down the hallway to the kitchen.

No Jewel.

Becoming more and more apprehensive, I started upstairs. Maybe she had decided to use the bathroom up there — although there was no reason to.

Before I even reached the top of the steps, I could see down the hallway that Jewel was standing in my bedroom. Her back was to me.

Moving quietly, ever so quietly, I crept down the hallway. Soon I was standing in my room behind Jewel.

It was true.

She was reading Laura's diary.

Chapter 25

Without a word I grabbed for the diary —
surprising Jewel. With the speed of a terrified
animal, she jumped, snatching the diary away
just as I was about to pull it out of her hands.

The sound of her shrieking pierced the air.

"What are you doing?" My own voice lashed
out, cracking through the room.

Jewel, holding the diary behind her, backed
away from me. Her eyes were wide with fear.
I moved closer as she continued edging away.

"Give me that!" I screamed. "How dare
you!"

I felt like a madwoman. Jewel was my friend.
I trusted her.

"How could you come sneaking in here,
trying to look at my diary! That's private!"

We stood there, red-faced, glaring at each
other. I was shaking with rage. Jewel was
shaking from shock and surprise.

"Just what were you doing looking in my diary, Jewel?" I asked quietly after I'd calmed myself down.

Jewel sat down on my bed. She hunched over and ran her fingers through her hair.

"Well, Delia. I know it doesn't look good."

"No. It doesn't look good at all."

Jewel was silent for a moment. "I don't know where to begin. I've been wanting to talk to you . . . Brock and I have both noticed how you've changed."

So now it's *Brock and I,* I thought. But aloud, I only said, "Go on."

"You're just not yourself. You change your appearance just about every minute. And you've got all these new clothes. You were never interested in clothes before."

"I'm just trying to . . . look my best." I realized that I'd almost said, *I'm just trying to get it right.*

Jewel stared at the floor. "It's not just the way you look. You're much more talkative. It's like you want to be the center of attention all the time. And then all of a sudden, you like to dance. . . ."

Jewel's voice trailed off.

"I think I get the idea, Jewel. I'm doing all these terrible things — like buying new clothes instead of wearing the same old jeans.

And I'm not wearing my hair the same way I did in grammar school. And I'm more outgoing. How terrible! Better go read my diary. Maybe you'll find out if I plan to buy a new pair of shoes. Is that what *you and Brock* were worried about?"

"Wait, Delia," Jewel protested. "It's not like that. I wasn't trying to do something . . . nasty." The words were tumbling out of her mouth. "It's just that I've been worried about you . . . about the way you've been acting. You just aren't the same anymore. You're like . . . like a different person."

Jewel looked up at me. "Delia, sometimes you act so — so strange. I just thought there might be something in your diary that would help me find out if something was going on. I thought I might learn something that would help me to *help you*."

Great. I had been worried that if I told Jewel my story she'd think I was crazy. I needn't have worried. She already thought I was crazy.

"You can't be angry with me, anyway," Jewel was saying, earnestly. She held the diary out to me, and I took it from her hand. "There's not one word in there. Nothing."

Chapter 26

There was an awful silence between us that seemed to have a life of its own.

Its presence hung in the air as Jewel left the house, and it lingered afterward.

I went downstairs to the den, and for a while I tried to study on my own for the history test. But trying to keep my mind focused was useless.

Then I sat on the couch and tried to watch television. That was no good, either. I couldn't even concentrate on the program.

I went back upstairs and threw the diary against the wall, wishing I had never seen it. As it fell behind my dressing table it knocked over the pink lamp I loved so much and broke it.

One more thing ruined by the diary. It had caused so much trouble.

It seemed so much fun to begin with, trying

out things I read about in the diary. And finding out about the girl who wrote it was like having a new friend.

But it wasn't fun anymore. As I'd gotten further into the diary, the pages had seemed to change. Laura's sense of humor got stranger and stranger. The things she thought were funny were downright mean . . . and sometimes gruesome. And those pranks of hers were getting sneakier and sneakier. They weren't things I wanted to try.

I told myself that I would just leave the diary where it had fallen behind my dresser. Perhaps it was a good idea not to read it for a while, anyway. I'd been altogether too involved in it.

I started to leave the room . . . but something pulled me back. *Jewel had said there wasn't one word in the diary.*

Why? I wondered. Did she think I'd be less angry if I thought she hadn't actually read anything? Or was she playing some kind of game — trying to make me believe I was crazy?

No, I decided. That was too farfetched.

Well, I thought . . . maybe she *didn't* read anything. Perhaps the first few pages didn't have any writing on them, and those were the only ones she'd seen. *That* must be what happened.

Was it?

But I couldn't remember if the first few pages were blank or not. And I had to find out.

So moments after I swore I'd leave the diary where it fell, I was bending over the dresser, searching behind it with my arm to find the diary.

"Gotcha!" I muttered as I fished the thing out.

Now I'll find out.

I undid the clasp.

I turned to the first page.

A smile spread over my face.

It was blank.

I turned to the next page. It was blank, too. And so was the next one.

Well, at least Jewel told the truth. And actually, I wasn't as angry as I would have been if she had read it.

I turned another page.

And my smile began to vanish.

It was blank.

Now my smile was gone.

The next page was blank.

And so was the one after that.

And the next. And the next.

Frantically, I kept turning page after page after page.

It was impossible, I told myself. How could everything have disappeared?

The pages in the diary *were* empty. Every single one.

My mind whirled in confusion. Was it possible that I had just imagined everything I had read? If that was true, then I *was* crazy.

I stared at the cover of the diary.

And then I stared some more.

Ah . . .

My shoulders sagged with relief. When Jewel and I were fighting, I hadn't *really looked* at the diary. Now that I had, I understood what I had been too upset to understand before.

From time to time I saw interesting diaries, and I bought them. It had become a hobby. And that way, I always had a new one handy, when I finished the old one.

This was just a diary I'd bought, and hadn't written in yet. Jewel must have picked it up off the shelf where I kept them. It wasn't *Laura's* diary at all.

Smiling, I opened the desk drawer where I'd left Laura's diary. Sure enough, it was there, safe and sound.

I opened it.

There were blank pages, just as I remembered. But the rest were filled with writing.

At the sight of the words on the pages, I gave a sigh of relief.

I don't know what made me do what I did next.

But I picked up a pen, intending to write on one of the blank pages.

As the pen touched the paper, it felt as if an unseen hand began to guide me. And then — it was as if I fell into a trance.

It was hours later when I finally emerged from that trance. When I did, the diary was on the floor at my feet. I bent down and retrieved it. Although I couldn't remember doing it, I must have been busy writing, for several pages were filled, now.

They all contained one sentence, written over and over again:

Find my killer.

Chapter 27

It was one of Mr. Parrish's writing assignments that helped me drop in another —
frightening — piece of the puzzle.

"We're going to start a new project today,
class," he started off the hour. "Something
that will give you a lot of room to use your
imagination."

There was shuffling of feet and the sound
of people shifting in their chairs. I loved Mr.
Parrish's offbeat assignments. They were
never the standard "read this and answer
questions" kind of fare. And he gave you a lot
of room to do something unique. Of course,
that meant it was harder to be lazy. Basically,
you either loved his class, or you hated it.

"We're going to go to the library and take
a look at some old newspaper stories. Natasha
will hand you each a roll of microfilm, with

several issues on it. Just take a look through it and see if a story interests you.

"It doesn't have to be a story that's a big deal, like an inauguration — in fact, sometimes a little story can be more interesting. And then, see what ideas you come up with — and write."

Mr. Parrish gave an exaggerated shrug and threw both hands in the air.

"Mr. Parrish, Mr. Parrish . . ." came a voice from the back of the room. I knew who it was — Stewart Smiley. Stewart always wanted the assignments to be more definite. "What exactly are we supposed to write?"

"Whatever you feel like, Stewart." Mr. Parrish smiled.

"But . . ." I turned around and saw that Stewart's face was etched with an expression he often wore after Mr. Parrish had given an assignment. It was somewhere between confusion and panic. Brock sat sprawled in a casual, almost insolent pose in the seat beside Stewart. He caught my eye and glared. I turned around quickly.

"Stewart — believe me. Whatever you do will be fine, as long as you give it an honest effort. Let's go."

We all trooped down to the library. Jewel

was beside me, while I could feel Brock's angry gaze on my back.

In the library, Natasha, the librarian, was waiting for us, armed with a box full of rolls of microfilm. I don't think any of us even knew what Natasha's last name was. She always told everyone to just call her Natasha. "Have fun," she said in a kidding tone. Then she winked.

"I won't," I replied, winking back. I moved to the microfilm machine and threaded in my film, adjusting the focus. I turned the knob and started to flip through the pages.

The newspaper I was viewing didn't exist anymore. It was called *The Pleasantville Tattler*. What in the world could there be to *tattle* about in Pleasantville? I wondered.

I flipped back and forth through the pages. Well — prices had certainly been much cheaper, I thought, looking at the clothing and makeup ads.

No wonder the *Tattler* went out of business, I said to myself after a few minutes. The paper seemed to focus on local news stories. Myrtle May Armbruster wins bakeoff competition. Calvin Whoople opens new fast food barbecue restaurant, the Saucy Pig.

"Got anything good?" Brenda Ann whispered.

"Negative."

Brenda Ann chuckled. "I think I'm going to have to write about a dog show."

Listlessly, I went back to turning the knob on my microfilm machine. After a few more minutes of looking at boring news items, I went to Natasha's office and asked if I could have a roll of microfilm with some different issue.

"You didn't find anything fascinating yet?" she grinned, flicking her dark hair over her shoulder. "I'm not surprised. Hold on a second while I get the key to the cabinet." While she fumbled through a drawer, a picture on her desk caught my eye. It was of a row of girls standing in front of a banner that said "Miss Teen Pleasantville." The picture must have been taken quite a while ago, because we didn't have a "Miss Teen Pleasantville" contest anymore.

The girl in the center was obviously the winner. She wore a red dress and carried a bouquet of roses. Something made me look more closely.

The girl in the picture had short hair. *Shockingly short.* The cut was similar to mine. In fact, mine was an updated version of the one she wore. I could see that the nails on the hands that held the roses were painted red.

I picked up the picture to look at it more

closely. There was something about it that was *so eerie.* It was almost like looking in a mirror. And yet, when I examined it, I could see that the girl's features weren't like mine at all. And the color of her hair was different. Hers was flaming red.

Then I realized where I'd seen that face before.

It was during the regression at Madam Randa's.

I had been somewhere in the past, in a room that I didn't recognize, and looked in the mirror at a face that wasn't mine.

It was the face of the girl in the photograph.

Chapter 28

Natasha saw me looking at the picture and gave me a wide smile. "There's my younger sister when she was in the Miss Teen Pleasantville contest, years ago," she said, pointing to a girl in a blue dress. "She should have been the winner, not that Laura Rawson." She nodded emphatically as she took the picture from my hand. She put it back on the desk next to a picture of herself in her skydiving gear.

The name Laura Rawson echoed in my mind. When I found the diary in my locker, I had thought the initials were LL or LR. The creeping sensation of dread that I had begun to feel grew stronger.

Natasha crossed her arms and gave a shrug. "Forget what I said. Laura never meant any harm. All she was interested in was boys and clothes . . . and writing in that diary of hers. And now she's dead."

"She's *dead?*"

"Drowned. Went swimming at night. She was always a wild one."

"Do you have anything about it — when she died, I mean?" I asked.

"Sure, it was a big story. Let me think, when was it?" Natasha tapped her forehead. "I think I know. Are you going to write about it for your class assignment?" she asked as we walked toward the microfilm cabinet.

"I guess so," I replied vaguely. My mind wasn't on the assignment right now.

It was on the picture of the girl in the red dress. Her hair was cut short like mine. Her nails were red, too . . . just like mine.

I had noticed that she was wearing red shoes, with bows. They looked just like the ones I had bought the other day. I could feel my palms starting to sweat. I promised myself that I would never, never wear the red shoes I had bought.

I stood there uneasily as Natasha unlocked the microfilm cabinet and started searching. "This must be it!" she said, holding a roll of microfilm out to me. "Here are two months worth of issues. The obituaries are somewhere toward the end of each issue, but you might as well just look on the front page. I remember they ran the story right after she died. Things like that don't happen around here every day." Natasha pressed her lips into a thin line.

"Thanks." I took the roll of film back to where I was sitting, and threaded it into the machine with trembling hands. I turned the knob on the machine quickly, searching for the article as fast as I could.

Then I saw the headline. *GIRL DIES IN FREAK ACCIDENT.*

There was a short article that told how Laura had gone swimming with a cousin in Albemarle Lake one night after a party. The cousin, whose family asked that her name be withheld, had tried to talk her out of it. She said Laura got a cramp, and she'd tried to save her, but the girl kept thrashing around so much that she couldn't.

I checked the date on the issue. May 9th. *My birthday.* The paper was from *eighteen years ago.*

My mouth had gone dry, and there was a roaring sound in my ears. Inside my head, a thought had begun to hammer insistently. The paper called her death a freak accident.

But I knew it wasn't an accident at all.

It was murder.

Chapter 29

The last thing I read in the article about Laura's death was that she'd been buried at Fairlawn Cemetery. The instant I knew that, I wished I didn't.

I was afraid to look at *her* grave. But now that I knew where Laura Rawson was buried, it was impossible to resist going there.

As soon as Mr. Parrish's class was over I left the school to go out to Fairlawn Cemetery. I didn't think twice about cutting classes anymore.

The librarian had given me directions to Fairlawn. It was a few miles outside of town, off the Old Post Road.

As I drove along, the sky took on an overcast hue. I kept wondering how I would feel when I looked at *my own tombstone*. I couldn't imagine it.

Soon I could see the cemetery up ahead.

As I got closer I could see that the grounds sloped gently downward from the road. Row upon row of headstones dotted the green grass. An eerie feeling wrapped around my heart, knowing that mine was among them.

I entered the cemetery through tall iron gates. A freakish thought entered my mind. They should have been *pearly gates*.

I parked the car and started to walk. I passed stone after stone, and monuments, some with statues of angels on them. A lump lodged in my throat as I saw some of the tiny ones . . . for children.

As I walked and walked, past row upon row of stones, I began to see that my task would be much more difficult than I had anticipated. Disappointment overtook me as I realized it could take days to locate the grave.

But then I spotted a workman wearing khaki trousers and a shirt with *Fairlawn Cemetery* printed on it. Perhaps he could help me. As I walked toward him I thought that it would feel strange to wear a shirt that said *cemetery* on it every day. But I supposed you got used to it. As I got nearer, I could see that he was digging a fresh grave.

"Excuse me, I'm looking for someone," I called out as I approached.

"Are they dead? I hope so," he answered, without looking up.

For a moment I was stunned by his remark. Then I realized he was making a joke.

"I'm looking for the grave of Laura Rawson."

The man still didn't look up. He kept digging as he said, "You should've asked over at the cemetery office. They've got a map in there that shows where everybody's buried."

"Oh," I said in a small voice, feeling even more disappointed. We were quite a ways away from the office.

"But," the man said as he leaned on his shovel, "it just so happens that I cleaned off some headstones a while ago, and I think one was hers." He pushed back his cap and mopped his forehead. "Two rows back, the white marble with the angel on top. You can't miss it."

I thanked the man and headed in the direction he had pointed. As I walked I felt a chill creeping into the air. I looked up and saw that it was getting cloudy.

Soon I was standing in front of the headstone, and I could read the name *Laura Rawson*. Underneath was a simple inscription, and the dates of her birth *and death. My birthday.*

As I stared, thoughts and images jumbled around in my mind.

What had the funeral been like? Had there been lots of people? Was there singing?

What kind of day had it been? Sunny, or raining? Perhaps it was overcast — like today.

I stood there for several moments. After a while I realized that I'd been crying. And then, I just couldn't stay there one more second. I ran, stumbling along, my vision blurred with tears. When I reached the car I jumped inside and sat there sobbing — not from sadness, but from being overcome with emotion.

I had just stood by the grave where *my own coffin* was buried under the ground. Inside it was *my own corpse.*

Chapter 30

When I got home from the cemetery, I took the painting I had turned to the wall and looked at it. Now I saw something I hadn't seen before. *The corpse was holding a diary in her hand. The same one I had been reading. The one I had seen first in a dream.*

Then I sat and thought.

There was no question about it. Any lingering traces of doubt had been banished from my mind. I had lived before, as Laura Rawson. And I had been murdered.

The person I had been was a girl with an outgoing, flamboyant personality. She could paint — and she also could lie, cheat, steal . . . and who knows what else? Her life had been cut short, and now she wanted it back. I was walking around with a split personality. One of them was living, and one was dead and wanted to live again.

I desperately wanted to remain myself, Delia. But could I?

At the end of every school year, an art show was held in the library. I decided to display the painting. If I had been driven to create it, perhaps it was meant to be seen. Perhaps if "Laura" got what she wanted, she would agree to rest.

When the day of the show came, everyone who passed by the painting stopped to look at it. Most of the time, there was a small crowd gathered around it, with people talking among themselves.

It even won first prize.

Normally, winning a prize would have thrilled me. But now I didn't know what to feel. In a way I *had* painted it, and in a way I hadn't.

Of course, I couldn't explain it to anyone. They'd think I was out of my mind. I nodded numbly to congratulations that I felt were undeserved. None, however, were from my closest friends.

I needn't have worried.

Brock walked by without a word. Brenda Ann wasn't there at all. And my encounter with Jewel wasn't very satisfying, either.

"Congratulations," she said. But Jewel's

smile looked pasted on. "You seem to get everything — without any effort at all."

"Well, you certainly don't sound too happy for me."

Jewel's expression was clouded. "I suppose in a way, I'm not. It's just that everything comes easy to you. You got a guy lots of girls were after — and you didn't even give it a thought. Then you decided you wanted to show me up in the fashion department . . . and you did. Now you win first prize in a show — and it's practically the first time you've even thought about art. Sure, Delia. I'm glad."

Then Jewel left, and I was alone again.

I felt a tap on my shoulder.

"Congratulations. You've surprised all of us." It was Mr. Parrish.

"Oh, thank you." Even though I didn't think I really deserved the congratulations, at this point I was just happy to hear a kind word.

"You know, I've been meaning to talk to you about the assignment you did about the newspaper story. But I'm surprised that you picked the one you did, and not something about the death of Laura Rawson. I saw you reading about it and you seemed so . . . involved. It seems like that would have been more interesting than the opening of the Saucy Pig Barbecue."

"Yes, but the story was — very disturbing," I managed to reply.

Mr. Parrish was silent for a moment. What he said next gave me an eerie feeling.

"I knew Laura Rawson. We were . . ."

"Mr. Parrish! Mr. Parrish!" someone called from across the room. It was Mr. Biddle, the computer teacher. He motioned Mr. Parrish toward him with a vigorous wave of his hand. "I want you to meet someone."

"Well — excuse me," Mr. Parrish said after hesitating for a moment. Then he turned and walked over toward Mr. Biddle, leaving me to wonder what he was going to say.

It was so . . . creepy. Why in the world hadn't it occurred to me before that I might know people who had known Laura? *Or had known me . . . before?*

I felt a tingle shoot down my spine as a host of questions crowded into my mind. How many other people did I know who had known Laura? Were any of them living a new life, as I was? Would we recognize each other? I hadn't recognized Mr. Parrish. Had he recognized me as Laura?

The questions flew around my head in a dizzying whirl. Finally it all became too overwhelming to contemplate. Somehow I managed to push all the questions to the back of my mind. I wanted to savor all the attention that the painting was receiving. It made me feel almost like a celebrity.

But my happiness was short-lived. By the next day, the painting had been slashed.

Chapter 31

Principal Tucker called me into his office to tell me the tragic news about the painting. He thought the slashing was a random act of vandalism.

Was it? I wondered. None of the other paintings had been touched. Why only mine?

Then I recalled my conversation with Mr. Parrish at the art show. What kind of relationship had he and Laura had? Was it possible that they had been enemies?

Even if they were, the thought of Mr. Parrish sneaking around at night and slashing up my painting seemed pretty unlikely. Still, I wanted to ask him about Laura. I planned to approach him after class that day.

But I didn't get the chance. Mr. Parrish seemed distracted during class — and then he left early. I hadn't counted on feeling so strange around him, either. It was going to be difficult to talk to him now that I knew he'd known Laura.

As the day went on, word about the painting got around. Wherever I went, condolences were offered.

"Tough about the painting. I hope they catch who did it."

". . . Real awful about the painting. Sorry."

"That really stinks. It was great."

I was getting some things out of my locker, when Jewel approached, tentatively.

"Delia . . . I wish I could take back the things I said yesterday. I felt terrible afterwards. And then when I heard about the painting, I felt even worse."

Jewel's eyes were red and swollen. I could tell that she'd been crying.

For a moment I wanted to tell her it was too late to be sorry. But then I remembered all the years we'd been friends, and how close we'd been.

"Well . . . we've been friends for a long time. Let's let bygones be bygones."

Jewel gave me a hug. "I'll call you later, okay?"

"Sure."

Jewel gave me another hug before she walked away. I stuck a few books in the locker, grabbed some other ones, and closed the door.

Brock was standing on the other side.

As our eyes met, I felt a surge of feeling inside.

"I'm sorry about what happened to your painting."

"Thanks."

We stood there in silence. Finally I turned to walk away.

"Wait." Brock put his hand on my arm. "I've really missed you, Delia."

His touch brought back so many memories. "I've missed you, too." Only then, I realized how much. At that moment I wanted to throw my arms around him. "I'm sorry I lied about going to college with you. I just didn't want us to fight."

Brock leaned against the locker and shrugged. "I understand. It's my fault, too, for pressuring you so much."

"You were so angry with me I thought I'd better stay away."

Brock sighed. "Nobody's perfect. I know I've got a bad temper. And I'm working on it, I really am. All I want is for us to make up."

I knew I wanted to say yes. But there was just a tiny bit of fear left. How could I be sure that Brock could control that temper of his?

As if Brock had read my thoughts he said, "For heaven's sake, Delia, I'm not a violent person. You've never known me to be violent, have you?"

That was true.

"Come on," Brock said, putting a hand on my shoulder. "Let's talk tonight — this evening. We can do whatever you want. Let's just . . . see each other."

"Okay," I said after a moment. "I'd like that. It doesn't matter what we do. I'd like to see you, too."

Brock looked thoughtful. "Let's just go for a ride."

As I drove home, my spirits were buoyant. Life seemed to be getting better again. My best friend and I had made up, and my boyfriend and I had gotten back together. If only I could be sure that I would no longer be troubled by "Laura."

Then I had an idea. I was almost home, but I turned the car around and headed for the Doorway to Beauty. I wanted to get my hair color changed. I wanted to look as little like Laura Rawson as possible.

I parked the car and hurried toward the Doorway to Beauty. But as I got closer, my heart sank. The shop looked empty. Maybe I was too late, and the shop was closed.

But the lights were on, and the CLOSED sign

wasn't on the door. I turned the handle and found the door was open. I went inside.

At first I thought Rose wasn't there. But then I saw her, sitting in a chair underneath one of the old-fashioned bubble top dryers, reading a magazine. The hair dryer wasn't on, but she was so absorbed in reading that she didn't hear me come inside.

"Rose?" I called softly, not wanting to startle her.

She looked up so calmly, as if she'd been expecting me.

As she looked up, I saw a scrap of material on the table beside her. It was pale blue, and had a ragged fringe.

I kept staring at it, not wanting to believe my eyes.

It was a scrap of canvas, torn from my painting.

Chapter 32

I stood there, terror-stricken, as Rose picked up the scrap of material and shook it.

And then it was as if the lens in each of my eyes turned and refocused. Rose wasn't holding a scrap of canvas. It was a dust rag.

I almost laughed with relief. How could I have let my imagination run away with me like that? The school was locked at night, anyway. There was no way Rose could have gotten inside.

"You don't look surprised to see me," I remarked as Rose put down her magazine. Though she smiled, I soon sensed that Rose wasn't looking at me. She was "looking through me," the way people sometimes do when they are lost in their own thoughts.

"Excuse me . . . Rose?" I said tentatively.

Rose blinked her eyelids in a quick flutter. "Oh! Delia, I was just off a million miles away!

It's been a long day and I was just about to close up. I was cleaning up and sat down to take a break and . . ." Her voice trailed off.

"Anyway, what can I do for you?" Rose glanced at the clock briefly and grinned at me. "Don't tell me you want a haircut! Your hair looks perfect, so don't ask me to do a thing to it."

I ran my hand against the crisp cut hairs at the nape of my neck. "It's not the cut, it's the color. Do you have time to dye my hair . . . right now . . . dye it brown?"

Rose looked shocked.

"Brown, Delia? You want me to dye it back to BROWN?"

She tilted her head to one side and threw both hands in the air.

"Everyone wants something *else*. Girls with curly hair want it straight, the ones with straight hair . . . they want it curly. Long hair they cut short, short hair they can't wait to grow. So I guess it's not strange that you should change brown to blonde and back to brown."

She looked at me sternly.

"Don't color your hair so much. It's not good for the hair."

"I won't," I told her. In fact I didn't think I'd ever change from my own hair color again.

I just couldn't wait to look like I used to —
not like the girl in the newspaper picture.

Rose eyed me thoughtfully. "Let's see . . .
your natural color is . . . a very dark, dark
shade of brown."

She picked up some fashion magazines and
flipped through them. When she found a model
with a nice shade of brown hair she showed
me the picture.

"Now *here's* the shade I think we should go
for." Rose held the open magazine out to me.

I gazed at the picture she pointed to.

"Yes. Like that," I agreed.

"Okay!"

Having decided it was a "go," Rose snapped
the magazine shut and handed me a smock.

"Go change, and we'll get started," she said,
pointing me toward the dressing room.

Soon I was changed and sitting in a chair
while Rose examined charts with little
swatches of fake hair in different colors.
"These tell me how to mix up the dye," she
explained.

Rose went to the back of the shop, took a
bottle off the shelf, and brought it back. I saw
that it was filled with dark brown liquid. She
emptied it into a plastic bowl.

"I heard what happened to your painting
over at school," Rose said as she stirred the

liquid into the bowl and mixed. "News travels fast in this town. What's the matter with people, anyway?"

I shrugged. I didn't want to talk about it.

In the mirror I could see Rose behind me, smiling as she brushed the dye onto my hair.

"You've got the right attitude. Just shrug it off and move on. Say — come to think of it, you look pretty happy, in spite of what happened. Got a new boyfriend or something?"

"It's the old one. He's back."

Now my head was covered with brown guck.

"Let's wait a few minutes."

Rose set a timer, and sat down in the chair beside me. I liked being in the shop, just Rose and me. It was like we were friends, and she was just doing my hair as a favor . . . and afterward I'd do hers. It was sort of like that.

I made a mental note to get some shorts and a shirt like the one she had on.

Rose went behind the reception desk and got a huge bar of chocolate. Unwrapping the foil, she broke off a square for herself and then held the bar out to me.

"So, this boyfriend's a good guy? Do I know who it is?"

"Umm . . . I don't know." I broke off a piece of chocolate. "Practically everybody in town knows each other, don't they? His name is Brock Davidson. His family lives on Crawley Street."

Rose frowned. "I think so, but I'm not sure. Wait . . . I think his sister gets her hair done here . . . is his sister's name Cheryl? She drives a little red car?"

I hoped I didn't have to have this gooey stuff on my head much longer. "No, Brock has a brother, but no sisters. He drives a black Mustang."

Rose nodded. "I know now. The Davidson brothers. Brock Davidson. Don't you think you ought to be careful about going out with him, Delia? Isn't he the one with the bad temper?"

The timer went off, making us both jump.

"Time to get that dye off your hair. Let's shampoo," Rose said, not waiting for me to comment on what she'd said about Brock. I was glad I didn't have to answer. His temper was the one thing about him that made me nervous. But after all . . . like Brock said, *nobody's perfect*.

"Any idea where you'll go on your date?" Rose asked as we walked to the shampoo sink.

"Oh, he said something about a romantic drive."

Rose nodded. "Just be careful."

I brushed her comments aside. Right now

I couldn't wait until I could see what the color looked like. I hoped I looked like *me* again.

After what seemed like forever in washing and conditioning and rewashing, Rose handed me a blow-dryer. "It's so late, I'd like to get things ready for tomorrow. Could you do me a favor and dry your hair? You know how you like it, anyway."

"Sure." I smiled, secretly happy Rose was asking me a favor. It made us seem more like friends.

So I started drying. And drying. Fortunately, with my hair so short, it wouldn't take long. I would only have to hurry a little bit to meet Brock.

The more I dried my hair, the more afraid I became. The color had looked brown when it was wet, but the more I dried it, the more it looked like . . . red.

I kept drying, praying for the color to change again.

Hoping didn't help. The dryer my hair got, the more it became red, *red*, RED.

How could it have happened?

"Rose! Rose!" I called.

Rose stopped as she got halfway to the chair, and put her hand to her mouth. Her face turned pale. "Oh, my . . . Delia. Look what happened."

"I can *see* what happened!" I wailed. "*How* did it happen? You must have made a mistake!"

Rose ran to the garbage can and picked out the empty dye bottle. "There's no mistake." She held the bottle out to me. As soon as I took it from her hand, she backed away, her face growing more ashen. "See for yourself. The bottle says it's *brown*. I've never seen anything like it," Rose said in a hushed voice. "It's kind of . . . spooky."

I examined the bottle. Sure enough, it said, *Ash Brown.*

But my hair was *flaming* red. Now I looked more like the girl in the picture than ever.

I was the very image of a dead girl.

Chapter 33

I was feeling sick. *Feeling sick, but looking dead,* I said to myself.

"Can't you fix it?" I asked Rose, hearing the desperation in my own voice.

Rose wasn't looking too well herself. That shade of pale was definitely not healthy for anyone who was alive. She was looking at me as if I were some sort of curiosity, and a scary one at that.

"There must be some explanation," she was saying as she clenched and unclenched her hands nervously.

"Rose, can you fix this?" I asked, more insistently.

Slowly, Rose walked over to me. "It's just . . . mystifying," she said as she examined my hair. "I've never seen anything like it."

"Please, Rose. We both know this wasn't

supposed to happen. But now, what can be done about it? I don't want this hair color. I don't want to look this way. . . ."

"I understand, Delia. I really do," Rose said in a professional tone of voice. "But there was brown dye in the bottle and now your hair is red, and I don't know why. I have to figure it out before I can figure out how to fix it."

Rose continued to examine my hair.

"Actually," she said, stooping down and examining me critically. "I think it looks better than brown. It really does. *It's really you.*"

That wasn't what I wanted to hear.

Rose stood up and walked a few steps away.

"Personally, as your stylist, I'd advise you to leave it the way it is." She paused for a moment. "Tell you what, see what your boyfriend thinks, how's that? You don't want me to start changing it now, do you? It's late."

I looked at the clock, miserable. "No."

I looked in the mirror again. I had to admit, that even though I didn't like what the color reminded me of, it *did* look good.

"No charge for this, of course. And if you decide you want me to fix it, there's no charge for that, either. This is just too . . ."

She didn't finish. *Weird,* was probably what she wanted to say.

I took a deep breath and got up from the chair.

"It *does* look good, Delia," Rose said as I took off the protective smock and gathered my things. "Maybe your hair was meant to be this color."

I looked up sharply. Rose was grinning, but I couldn't manage a smile. I didn't think this was something to joke about.

There was an uncomfortable silence, and then I said good-bye to Rose. As soon as I left, she turned the CLOSED sign on the door of the shop around, facing out.

I hoped we were still going to be friends.

"Wow!!" was all Brock said when he picked me up. It took him at least a full minute to say "I love your hair." During the minute, I wondered what "wow" meant.

As we drove along, the soft spring breeze blew against the window, making me think of the summer that stretched out ahead.

"You know, I wanted to get a chance to be alone with you, so I could explain the way I've been acting." Brock stared straight ahead at the road as he spoke. "Jewel tells me she thinks you're afraid of going to college. Not that I'm saying I think it's true," he said hurriedly, before I had voiced my objection.

"All I'm saying is that . . . it's true for me. Sure, I'm a little scared. I've lived in this Small Town, U.S.A. all my life. Where I'm going, well, Harrison's a big school. Who knows what the future holds?"

Brock laughed. It sounded nervous and tinny. After a moment of silence he continued. "For a long time I told myself that I wasn't afraid of anything. And I almost got myself to believe it. But then, I couldn't any longer."

Brock glanced at me out of the corner of his eye for a moment, before staring back at the road.

We drove along in silence for a few minutes. I could see Brock steal an occasional glance at me out of the corner of his eye.

"So what I'm getting at is," Brock went on, "that when I had to admit that I was scared, I thought having you along would make it easier."

Now that Brock had admitted he was scared, I was beginning to see that perhaps Jewel was right all along. Maybe I *was* scared after all.

"Well, who knows what's going to happen with school?" I said. I decided not to mention that I'd been thinking of going to art school.

"Yes — who knows what's going to happen,

after all?" Brock said. The hushed tone of his voice startled me. "You know, Delia, it's hard to think of you going to another school . . . without me. Dating someone else. . . ."

Brock let out a long, deep sigh. "This has got to stop," he said quietly, as if talking to himself.

I saw that Brock's hands were clutching the steering wheel so tightly that the knuckles were white. He seemed lost in thought.

"This has got to stop," he said again, in a hushed whisper.

I could barely hear him.

The sun had set, and a full moon had begun to rise. I glanced at my watch, and saw that the little numbers on the face were beginning to glow a little. Brock had picked me up over an hour ago.

We whizzed by a road sign. I squinted in an effort to read it, but couldn't make it out.

"Brock?" I touched his arm. "Where are we going?"

Brock stared straight ahead. He seemed a million miles away.

"Brock," I said, raising my voice half an octave, "would you please tell me where we're going?"

Brock shook his head slightly.

"So," I persisted. "Where are we going?"

Brock's voice was soft, teasing. "It's a surprise." But when I turned to look at Brock his
expression wasn't teasing, or playful. I couldn't
even describe it — except that he looked . . .
frightening.

Chapter 34

I prayed that my imagination was playing tricks on me, but, try as I might, I couldn't convince myself. Brock seemed stranger by the minute — as if he'd become someone else. I remembered what I'd read once about serial killers — how they could be very charming and suddenly — they changed.

And then Brock said something that nearly made my heart stop beating.

"I want to show you Albemarle Lake. A girl died there years ago — or so I've heard."

"Brock, you must be kidding," I said, trying to keep the edge of fear out of my voice. "Why would I want you to take me on a guided tour of the place where this girl died?"

Brock shrugged. "Oh, come on, Delia. That was a long time ago. It's just that I know you'd love seeing the lake at night. The moon is out . . . it's so — peaceful."

The light of the full moon shone through the trees. It illuminated the edges of Brock's face and hair with a halo-like glow.

"Can you imagine, Delia — what it must be like by the lake, in this moonlight? You know what would be great? To go swimming at night, in the lake. You might never get another chance to do something like that again."

You might never get another chance . . .

His words echoed in my ears.

I had a crystal-clear moment of insight that flashed through me with piercing intensity. The image of the very first diary page I'd ever "read" appeared in my mind's eye.

Let me tell you how I died. I remember seeing blood before my eyes. At first I thought I was floating in blood, but then I understood that I was lying in water. . . .

I shut my eyes tightly, wanting to block out the image of the page. But it remained, carved into my memory.

. . . I knew that it was my own blood, but strangely enough, that didn't bother me. I felt quite calm and peaceful.

That's when I realized that I wasn't breathing anymore.

I understood everything, now. I had died in a swimming "accident." But it was no accident.

I was murdered.

I looked at Brock's shimmering profile. What if murderer and victim had found each other once again? Now I had a chance to save myself. If I didn't . . . would I just keep circling around again and again, meeting the same fate over and over?

I moved my hand so that it rested on the door handle. But I knew there was no chance of jumping out. We were moving much too fast.

A turnoff was coming up. I prayed that Brock would turn around and we'd head back to Pleasantville.

I held my breath.

An impact from behind the car hurled me against the door so hard that the wind was knocked out of me. Only the seat belt prevented me from bouncing into the dashboard.

"Hey, are you crazy?" Brock yelled to the image in the rearview mirror.

BLAM! Another impact sent the car hurling forward. I stopped with a jerk as the seat belt checked my motion, pulling me up short as it tightened against my chest.

"Hey, are you drunk?" Brock yelled at the rearview mirror again. He gripped the steering wheel tightly as he fought to keep the car moving straight ahead on the road. I tried to get a glimpse of the car in the mirror, but it was already moving alongside of us, low and sleek, the gray color blending into the shadows of the night. It was barely visible in the darkness.

I heard a shriek of metal scraping against metal. The car was bumping us from the side, now.

I could see beads of sweat glistening on Brock's forehead. "We've got ourselves a real nut, here," he said.

"Why would anyone do this?" I whispered.

"I don't know." Brock clenched his jaw tightly. "I can't imagine anybody crazy enough to . . ."

Brock's words were sliced off in midair by another jolt from the gray car. Whoever it was meant business. The impact sent us rocketing onto the shoulder of the road, into the soft dirt. Brock turned the wheel, and we were back on the roadway again, only to receive another shot from the ghostly gray car.

The road was deserted and the trees loomed, menacing, on either side of us. This is killer country, I thought to myself, looking at the surrounding woods.

Another bump from the gray car.

I looked toward the car and tried to see inside. But all I could see was a figure hunched over the steering wheel in a hooded coat that completely covered the face.

"Okay, no more Mister Nice Guy," Brock said through clenched teeth. "Hang on, it's going to be a bumpy ride."

I could feel that temper of his gathering itself full force. The anger radiated from him like heat from a blast furnace.

Brock stepped down hard on the accelerator. Bumpy was right. Flying pieces of gravel shot up from the road. The car shuddered as it connected with each pothole. Sometimes we skidded on patches of sand.

The next time the gray car edged over to bump us, Brock turned the wheel sharply to the left and bumped first.

The action seemed to take the driver of the other car by surprise. For a moment the gray car wavered unsteadily. Then it swerved crazily all over the road. It was apparent that the driver had lost control. We sped ahead and were able to gain several car lengths.

Brock smiled and tapped the horn lightly. "Hey, dirtbag!" he said, grinning as if he'd beaten the other driver in a game.

But this was a very deadly game.

The other driver regained control. I could see the car's headlights fast approaching in the rearview mirror. We were being chased again.

It seemed that fate had created a foolproof plan for my death. No matter what I tried to do, history would repeat itself tonight, and I would be killed.

Brock tried speeding up again, but his car was no match for the gray one. "I'll show you, you little twerp," he muttered as the car moved in closer. He swerved to the left again, but this time the gray car turned more quickly, and sharply. I felt the traction of the wheels starting to slip across the road. I could tell that the car was heading into a spin, and that Brock was trying to turn into it. Everything seemed to speed up and slow down at the same time.

The car started to turn. The dark woods whirled around me with dizzying speed, faster and faster. Then there was a crash of metal and glass, followed by an enormous jolt. It was like falling off the edge of the world.

As I plunged into the blackness, the last thing I heard was the horn blaring into the night.

Chapter 35

I was sinking down into the water, and the red was swirling around me. That's when death came. I could feel a pain in my stomach — a cramp. The pain was so bad, every time I tried to swim, I doubled over and then my head went under water.

That was how I came to die.

But no — that wasn't exactly it. There was something missing.

There was someone behind me.

I knew who it was — but I just can't remember. It was someone I felt close to . . . very close.

Then they hit me with something . . . a rock, I think . . . and my head exploded with pain. I couldn't think of anything else. The pain shot out through my head and into my body. Great, shooting stars of pain so powerful that I couldn't remember anything anymore.

*   *   *

The diary was floating in space, right before my eyes.

I turned the last page as a noise pulled me back to consciousness.

It was the car horn, I realized as I sat up.

Where was I?

I looked outside into the blackness of the night.

My whole body ached. Gently, I moved my legs.

Slowly, I sat forward.

The memory of being chased by the gray car came flooding back — as a sharp pain shot through my arm. I had bent it in front of me as I fell toward the dashboard. The seat belt pulled me back, but the impact had been so sharp that my arm had struck the dash. I flexed it gently.

It was badly bruised, but not broken, I thought. Then I saw Brock, slumped against the steering wheel.

Trembling, I reached out and put my hand on his forehead. It was hot. I touched his neck, and soon found his pulse, beating strong.

Brock had meant to kill me. I was sure of it. That's why he'd brought me out here — to the same place I died so many years ago — in another life. If he killed me, he wouldn't have to go away and leave me. He wouldn't have to think of me going out with someone else.

But someone had run us off the road.

A tapping against the window made me jump.

I looked toward the sound, and for a moment I saw nothing. Then I made out the black-clothed figure that seemed like a gigantic black widow spider in the darkness.

Had I eluded Brock's plan, only to meet death in the woods at the hands of an anonymous killer?

Why did the figure just stand there watching me . . . like a spider waiting for a fly to enter the web?

"Are you hurt?" the hooded figure asked.

I remembered the doors were locked. And locked they'll remain I said to myself.

I was sick with fear. I wondered if the black cloaked figure would break into the car and kill us both, perhaps with an axe.

"Open the door."

I sat perfectly still.

Then the figure removed its hood, and my heart leaped with joy.

"Rose!" I said. I couldn't remember being so glad to see anyone.

Hurriedly I unbuckled my seat belt and fumbled with the door handle. It was stuck and wouldn't open.

"Roll down the window," Rose called, making a turning motion with her hand.

I rolled down the window and climbed up onto the seat. Then I gingerly put my head and shoulders through the opening. Balancing myself with my hands, I slowly edged my way outside.

Fortunately, I'm very flexible, and when my head and shoulders were outside the window, I was able to lift myself up and, with Rose's help, maneuver the rest of my body to the ground.

I wrapped my arms around Rose, so happy to be alive that I didn't care that I was disheveled and bruised.

"How did you know he was going to come out here? You told me to be careful . . . and then you came to save me . . . how did you know?" I babbled as Rose and I hugged each other.

"Never mind . . . I just had a hunch. You told me you were going out for a drive, and so I waited outside your house until you got into the black Mustang . . . and then I followed you.

"I had a feeling you'd end up here by the lake."

Chapter 36

"That's amazing!" I said. "How on earth did you guess?"

"I just . . . I just knew," Rose said, simply. "Come on, let's walk."

In a kind of a daze, I followed. "I was afraid he was trying to kill me."

Rose continued to walk.

"Shouldn't we try to flag someone down?" I called to her. "Brock probably needs help. He might be badly hurt."

Rose was walking on ahead of me, alongside the road. I hurried on behind her. When I finally caught up to her I repeated what I'd said about Brock.

"You still keep worrying about him. That's a surprise."

A tree branch snapped under my feet. Rose kept moving steadily up ahead of me. I could tell that we were heading further into the woods. Now it occurred to me that perhaps Brock wasn't the only one who had been injured just now. Maybe something had happened to Rose.

"Rose! Turn around! You're heading away from the road!" I called.

Rose stopped. I saw her straighten up . . . but then she kept on walking. My sense of relief was beginning to evaporate. What if I was stuck out here in the woods alone with *two* accident victims? The thought sent a flash of panic tearing through my exhausted mind.

"Rose, please turn around!" For a moment Rose paid no attention. She continued to keep walking. But then, sensing that no one followed, she stopped again. I rejoiced as I saw her turn around.

I hugged myself in a useless effort to bring some warmth into my body. "Did something happen?" I asked as Rose drew nearer. "When you stopped the car, did you hit your head?"

Rose put her hand on my arm. She began to giggle — an eerie, shrill sound in the lonely woods. "Did I hit my head?" She began to laugh. I could see her body shake.

I sensed that something was wrong, and it created the kind of feeling that comes over you when you lose your balance . . . and you're going to fall. In that split second, you pray that somehow you can regain your footing . . . and avoid the inevitable tragedy of hitting the ground and the injury that happens along with it.

It's in that split second that you know your fate turns. It was in that split second that I saw Rose's face, and I knew I was hurtling into disaster.

She threw back her head, and kept laughing. Still laughing, she looked at me, her eyes like two great glittering pits.

"Hello again, Laura," she whispered.

It was then I understood everything.

Rose was completely insane.

Her grip tightened on my arm. Though I tried with all my strength, I knew it was useless to pull away from her.

We stumbled along, Rose half pushing me and half dragging me through the woods. The straps of my sandals cut into my feet — but soon there were no sandals left. They had been pulled from my feet by the tangled underbrush.

There was no question of getting away from Rose. She was full of frenzied strength, while it took everything I possessed to keep from falling down. If I did, she would have dragged me along, I was sure of it.

As we plunged along, Rose spoke to me incessantly. "Why'd you have to come back after so many years? You should have left well enough alone, Laura." Rose gave me a tremendous pull that nearly jerked my arm from its socket.

"I recognized you that first night in the classroom, in spite of your plain Jane disguise. I could hardly keep from jumping up and pointing a finger at you, the way you sat there like butter wouldn't melt in your mouth."

Rose turned to look back at me, exposing her teeth in a hideous grin. "I might've known you'd get cute, coming around the shop with your little games. Cutting your hair like you used to . . . using the same kind of nail polish. You couldn't come right out and just say, 'remember me?' "

"Rose, you're not making sense. I'm not who you think I am," I protested. But of course, I knew it was no use.

"I thought maybe when you saw that diary, you'd know I was on to you," Rose hissed. "Maybe then you'd think twice about tangling with me again."

Rose stopped, and I had barely enough breath left in me to utter the words, "You put it there? But how?"

The smile of satisfaction on Rose's face was

grotesque. "I still had the key to the school from when I taught the Doorway to Beauty course at night. I always watched when you went home, so I knew which locker was yours. Breaking into it was real easy."

With mounting horror I realized that Rose had watched me for a long time. Much longer than I had suspected. She had stalked me through many days when I imagined myself happy and carefree.

Long before I had dreamed of the diary, and my fears had taken hold of me, she had been watching . . . and waiting.

"You should have known better than to try to fool cousin Rosie."

Rose was shaking her head back and forth.

"Now you're going to have to learn all over again that I'm not your Goody-Two-Shoes."

In stunned terror I realized who the insane individual that stood before me was. *Cousin* Rose.

Goody-Two-Shoes.

How could I explain to another human being what it is to find oneself the star of one's own private horror story . . . where the knowledge that the impossible has become possible goes hand in hand with the understanding that death is near?

As I grasped the reality of Rose's identity,

I realized that for some time I had been hearing the sound of water. Rose and I had wandered close to the banks of the lake.

"Look familiar?" Rose asked, with a death-mask grin.

Yes, it did.

I was murdered here once.

And I might be murdered here again.

Chapter 37

I rushed at Rose with all of my remaining strength. In the core of my mind I thought that my only hope was to push her into the lake . . . to push her, before she pushed me.

But it was impossible to anticipate the shifting of the wet shore. At the last moment, my foot sank into a pocket of water just beneath the mud, and I lurched sideways, nearly losing my balance. My hands struck Rose's body and slid away with a fraction of the force I had put behind them. Rose lost control for barely an instant, and then grabbed at me with both hands, catching me around the neck. She twisted and threw me toward the edge of the lake.

I was helpless to prevent myself from hurtling straight into the water. It struck me right in the face as I fell, surging into my nose and mouth and into my eyes.

By some miracle I gained my footing and turned in time to see Rose coming at me . . . with a rock in her hand. I saw the rock descending as if in slow motion, closer and closer. . . .

As the rock was about to strike, somehow I swerved. The rock grazed my head slightly as the momentum carried Rose forward. Before she regained her balance, I grabbed her wrist and pulled the rock out of her hand. Then I raised the rock high over my head and threw it as far away as I could.

The rock had barely left my hand when I felt something hurl against me under the water. It was Rose, trying to knock my feet out from under me.

I tried to keep my balance, but my feet were sliding in the soft, muddy bottom of the lake. Once more I plunged headfirst into the water, choking and gasping for air.

This time, I refused to allow terrifying memories to intrude on my thinking. I knew I needed to focus one hundred percent of my entire being on surviving right now.

Rose was pushing down hard on my back, trying to hold me under. Rather than pushing against her, I made myself dive down further, letting the force Rose was using to push me, carry her into the water instead.

As I felt her falling, I propelled myself out from under her and surged upward. I only had a moment to gulp a breath of air. Then I turned to find Rose's body before she could resurface. Now *I* was the one holding *her* under.

I had no real thought of what I was doing anymore. I was operating on pure animal survival instinct, fighting to stay alive by any means necessary.

For an instant I felt Rose stop struggling. Her body went limp. But she was only acting to throw me off guard — to gain an advantage that enabled her to twist away from me.

We struggled back and forth in the water, each one of us gaining and losing the upper hand by turns. Somehow, I was finally able to maneuver myself onto the bank, and I tried to run. But Rose was too quick, and soon caught me. We continued to struggle . . . for how long, I don't know. I was past the point of exhaustion when I saw Rose, fueled with the energy of the insane, preparing for another attack.

Barely able to stand, I summoned a force from somewhere within and propelled myself forward, arms outstretched, toward her. I struck her with both my outstretched arms. Caught off guard, she fell backward into the mud on the bank of the lake.

The moon was glittering through the trees. For several moments I stared at Rose's motionless form, shimmering in the moonlight. *She tried to kill me,* I said over and over to myself. *She tried to kill me.*

Just then a blinding light enveloped everything around me. I looked up and was able to make out something in the sky.

"It's a helicopter," I realized, giggling hysterically. For some reason it struck me as insanely funny.

"Delia, over here," someone called out.

Numbly, I looked around.

Standing there, looking ghostly in the mixture of light from the moon and the helicopter searchlight, was Brock.

The noise of the helicopter circling overhead provided a backdrop for the next chaotic moments. A jeep bearing the insignia of the Pleasantville Police Department had somehow made it through the woods. The beam of the headlights shone in our eyes as it pitched to a halt in a nearby clearing. Police officers jumped out and ran toward Brock, Rose, and me as another jeep followed.

An officer pulled Rose to her feet. She was covered with mud. But I knew I looked no better.

"Come on, come this way . . . follow me."

An officer was talking to me gently, guiding me to one of the jeeps. Brock followed. Soon we were wrapped in blankets, sitting in the back of one of the police jeeps.

My teeth chattered. It felt as if I would never get rid of the chill. I would feel cold for the rest of my life.

I looked at Brock sitting next to me, and reached out and took his hand.

"Thank goodness you found us," I said to the officers in the front seat. "But . . . what brought you up here?"

"We got a tip from a teacher . . . what's his name?"

"Charlie Parrish," his partner responded. "It seems that Charlie went for a haircut, and Rose started sounding like she'd flipped. She was saying some really crazy things about having to hurry because she had to go kill her cousin. Charlie knew the cousin had been dead for years. He said she was his high school sweetheart.

"But Rose told him she wasn't dead anymore. And now she was calling herself Delia Monroe."

Chapter 38

Rose told the whole story when we got to the police station. I had no choice but to listen to her tell it. The only way she would confess was if she was allowed to tell her story directly to "Laura," who she was convinced had come back to haunt her.

It took nearly two hours to get the full story from Rose, in stumbling, disjointed speech. But finally, the whole story of how she, Charlie Parrish, and Laura had been students at Harding High emerged. She had suffered insult after insult at Laura's hands.

"You always got away with everything — sneaking out at night, cheating on your school-work, wearing makeup when it wasn't allowed. You were always popular no matter what mischief you caused. I was always your goody-goody cousin, especially after you started calling me that name, 'Goody-Two-Shoes.' "

When Laura challenged her to go swimming in Albemarle Lake one night, Rose accepted, even though she was scared.

"Then you got a cramp."

Rose smiled a little . . . if what she did could really be called a smile. It was more of a grimace.

"I knew the cramp was a sign, as if somehow I was being told, 'Look, see how easy it will be? Just finish the job.' And so I picked up the rock . . ."

Rose was quiet for a moment before she continued. "Everybody believed me when I said I tried to save you. I'd never been bad before. They all told me how sad it was that I had to watch my cousin drown. I was the only one that knew *why you had to die*."

"WHY?" I asked, desperately.

Rose looked at me with an expression so fierce that a detective put a restraining hand on her shoulder. "I was the only one who knew you were dangerous. I knew you dug up the holes in the front yard and covered them with leaves so Grandma would turn her ankle."

Rose crossed her arms and began rocking back and forth. "Oh, I knew about all of those bad *accidents* that you caused. Just like I knew you were crazy. I used to read your diary all the time."

Chapter 39

Dear Diary,

I'm not afraid of the future anymore. And I no longer feel as if there's a struggle between a living personality and a dead one going on inside me. Here at art school I've started a whole new life, and tried to put those awful memories behind me.

Now that I've lived through that whole terrible episode, I find I feel stronger than I've ever felt before. In fact, in a strange way, I think some good came out of the whole nightmare.

For instance, I pay more attention to my appearance. If it hadn't been for the diary, I never would have known that I like red nail polish. Sometimes I think I'll try another color, but for now, I'm sticking to red.

I've decided that I like my hair this way, and

I like it red, too. I think I'm going to keep it like this. My new boyfriend loves it. <u>He thinks it's really me.</u>

It's too bad about Aunt Gracie, though. The way she died, in that bad accident.

Also in the *Point Horror* series

POINT CRIME

If you like Point Horror, you'll love Point Crime!

A murder has been committed . . . Whodunnit?
Was it the teacher, the schoolgirl, or the best friend? An exciting new series of crime novels, with tortuous plots and lots of suspects, designed to keep the reader guessing till the very last page.

Kiss of Death
School for Death
Peter Beere

Avenging Angel
Final Cut
Shoot the Teacher
David Belbin

Baa Baa Dead Sheep
Jill Bennett

A Dramatic Death
Margaret Bingley

Driven to Death
Anne Cassidy

Overkill
Alane Ferguson

Death Penalty
Dennis Hamley

The Smoking Gun
Malcolm Rose

Look out for:

Concrete Evidence
Malcolm Rose

The Beat:
Missing Persons
David Belbin

Break Point
David Belbin

Accidents Will Happen
Chris Westwood

Point

Pointing the way forward

More compelling reading from top authors.

The Highest Form of Killing
Malcolm Rose
Death is in the very air . . .

Seventeenth Summer
K.M. Peyton
Patrick Pennington – mean, moody and out of control . . .

Secret Lives
William Taylor
Two people drawn together by their mysterious pasts . . .

Flight 116 is Down
Caroline B. Cooney
Countdown to disaster . . .

Forbidden
Caroline B. Cooney
Theirs was a love that could never be . . .

Hostilities
Caroline Macdonald
In which the everyday throws shadows of another, more mysterious world . . .

POINT SF

Encounter worlds where men and women make
hazardous voyages through space; where time travel is a
reality and the fifth dimension a possibility; where the
ultimate horror has already happened and mankind
breaks through the barrier of technology . . .

The Obernewtyn Chronicles:
Book 1: Obernewtyn
Book 2: The Farseekers
Isobelle Carmody
A new breed of humans are born into a hostile world
struggling back from the brink of apocalypse . . .

Random Factor
Jessica Palmer
Battle rages in space. War has been erased from earth and is
now controlled by an all-powerful computer – until a random
factor enters the system . . .

First Contact
Nigel Robinson
In 1992 mankind launched the search for extra-terrestial
intelligence. Two hundred years later, someone responded . . .

Virus
Molly Brown
A mysterious virus is attacking the staff of an engineering plant
. . . Who, or *what* is responsible?

Look out for:

Strange Orbit
Margaret Simpson

Scatterlings
Isobelle Carmody

Body Snatchers
Stan Nicholls

Read Point SF and enter a new dimension . . .

Point R♥mance

Look out for this heartwarming Point Romance
mini series:

First Comes Love
by Jennifer Baker

Can their happiness last?

When eighteen-year-old college junior Julie
Miller elopes with Matt Collins, a wayward and
rebellious biker, no one has high hopes for a
happy ending. They're penniless, cut off from
their parents, homeless and too young. But no
one counts on the strength of their love for one
another and commitment of their vows.

Four novels, *To Have and To Hold, For Better
For Worse, In Sickness and in Health,* and *Till
Death Do Us Part,* follow Matt and Julie through
their first year of marriage.

Once the honeymoon is over, they have to deal
with the realities of life. Money worries,
tensions, jealousies, illness, accidents, and the
most heartbreaking decision of their lives.
Can their love survive?

Four novels to touch your heart . . .

Point Romance

Caroline B. Cooney

The lives, loves and hopes of five young girls appear in this dazzling mini series:

Anne – coming to terms with a terrible secret that has changed her whole life.

Kip – everyone's best friend, but no one's dream date . . . why can't she find the right guy?

Molly – out for revenge against the four girls she has always been jealous of . . .

Emily – whose secure and happy life is about to be threatened by disaster.

Beth Rose – dreaming of love but wondering if it will ever become a reality.

Follow the five through their last years of high school, in four brilliant titles: *Saturday Night, Last Dance, New Year's Eve,* and *Summer Nights*

Point Romance

If you like Point Horror, you'll love Point Romance!

Anyone can hear the language of love.

Are you burning with passion, and aching with desire? Then these are the books for you! Point Romance brings you passion, romance, heartache . . . and *love*.

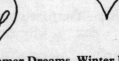

Available now:

First Comes Love:
To Have and to Hold
For Better, For Worse
In Sickness and in Health
Till Death Do Us Part
Jennifer Baker

A Winter Love Story
Jane Claypool Miner

Two Weeks in Paradise
Denise Colby

Saturday Night
Last Dance
New Year's Eve
Summer Nights
Caroline B. Cooney

Cradle Snatcher
Kiss Me, Stupid
Alison Creaghan

Summer Dreams, Winter Love
Mary Francis Shura

The Last Great Summer
Carol Stanley

Lifeguards:
Summer's Promise
Summer's End
Todd Strasser

French Kiss
Robyn Turner

Look out for:

Crazy About You
Robyn Turner

Spotlight on Love
Denise Colby

Last Summer, First Love:
A Time to Love
Goodbye to Love
Jennifer Baker

POINT FANTASY

Read Point Fantasy and escape into the realms of the imagination; the kingdoms of mortal and immortal elements. Lose yourself in the world of the dragon and the dark lord, the princess and the mage; a world where magic rules and the forces of evil are ever poised to attack . . .

Available now:

Doom Sword
Peter Beere
Adam discovers the Doom Sword and has to face a perilous quest . . .

Brog The Stoop
Joe Boyle
Can Brog restore the Source of Light to Drabwurld?

The "Renegades" series:
Book 1: Healer's Quest
Book 2: Fire Wars
Jessica Palmer
Journey with Zelia and Ares as they combine their magical powers to battle against evil and restore order to their land . . .

Daine the Hunter:
Book 1: Wild Magic
Book 2: Wolf Speaker
Tamora Pierce
Follow the adventures of Daine the hunter, who is possessed of a strange and incredible "wild magic" . . .

POINT FANTASY

Point Horror Fans Beware!

Available now from Point Horror are tales for the midnight hour...

THE *Point Horror* TAPES

Two Point Horror stories are terrifyingly brought to life in a chilling dramatisation featuring actors from The Story Circle and with spine tingling sound effects.

Point Horror as you've never heard it before...

HALLOWEEN NIGHT
FUNHOUSE

available now on audiotape at your nearest bookshop.

Listen if you dare...